THE RED BADGE OF COURAGE

AN EPISODE OF THE AMERICAN CIVIL WAR

by

Stephen Crane

adapted by

Margaret Tarner

MACMILLAN

First published 1987
Reprinted 1990

Published by MACMILLAN EDUCATION LTD
London and Basingstoke
*Associated companies and representatives in Accra,
Auckland, Delhi, Dublin, Gaborone, Hamburg, Harare,
Hong Kong, Kuala Lumpur, Lagos, Manzini, Melbourne,
Mexico City, Nairobi, New York, Singapore, Tokyo.*

ISBN 0-333-43583-4

Printed in Hong Kong

PREFACE

Stephen Crane was born in America in 1871, and died in Germany in 1900. In 1895, he wrote his best known novel, *The Red Badge of Courage,* a study of the heart and mind of a new recruit to the army of the Union, during the American Civil War of 1861–1865. He was not born till after this war was over, and he had never seen a battle. Yet the book is one of the most realistic war novels ever written.

His youthful hero, Henry Fleming, enlists with high hopes of glory, yet, as soon as he goes to the front, doubts and fears trouble him—just as they have troubled most new recruits in every country since wars began. In fact, Henry represents youth in war.

The book has the sub-title, *An Episode of the American Civil War.* That is all it is—an episode lasting just a few days during one of the many long battles of the war.

All forms of war are brutal, and none more so than civil war. During the American Civil War, over half a million lives were lost. This horrifying fact can be more easily believed when one reads Stephen Crane's imaginative account of a brief episode in the struggle which lasted five years.

There is also a degree of futility in war. This is well illustrated in the book by the ironic touch of beginning and ending the episode with the same observation by the men: 'We're going to come in round behind 'em.' No wonder the youthful hero doubted the wisdom of those in command. There is also irony in the manner in which the hero acquires his own red badge of courage.

Nevertheless, the American Civil War was an event of the greatest significance, not only to America but to the whole world. By their victory over the Southern States, the Northern States of the Union secured the abolition of slavery, and prepared the way for the emancipation of the black population. The President of the Union, Abraham Lincoln, in his victory address after the Battle of Gettysburg in 1863, used the immortal words, 'Government of the people, by the people, for the people'. This is a message still repeated by leaders of all states, the world over, where democracy is the accepted form of government.

This is a retold version of Stephen Crane's story, written in simple modern English. The original book is full of imagery and poetic expressions, and abounds in fanciful turns of phrase, now rather outdated and difficult to understand. In this version, the story of Henry's part in the battle, and his relationship with some of his comrades, are emphasised and closely followed. It is hoped that this will provide a tale to interest those who enjoy adventure stories with a historical background.

M. G.

Chapter 1

As the night ended, the cold passed **reluctantly** from the earth, and the morning mists cleared to reveal an army stretched out on the hills, resting.

As the landscape changed from brown to green, the army awoke and began to stir in eagerness at the sound of voices and rumours. It cast its eyes upon the roads, which were beginning to show up as proper roadways instead of the long ruts of liquid mud that had gleamed before in the darkness. A river, shining amber in the shadow of its banks, ran along its course almost at the army's feet. This water had become a dull blackness at night, when the distant red gleam of enemy camp fires had shone from the distant hills.

One of the soldiers went to the river to wash a shirt. He came flying back, waving the garment like a banner. He was full of a tale he had heard from a reliable friend, who had heard it from a truthful cavalry-man, who had heard it from his trustworthy brother, who was one of the **orderlies** at Division Headquarters. He told the news as if he was a **herald of signal importance**:

'We're going to move tomorrow—sure,' he said to a group of his section. 'We're going 'way up river, then cut across and come in round behind 'em.'

To his audience he drew a loud and detailed plan. When he had finished, the blue-uniformed men broke into scattered groups, arguing as they stood between the rows of low brown huts. A Negro who had been dancing upon a wooden box in front of a number of the soldiers was left deserted. He sat **mournfully** down. Smoke drifted lazily from the quaint chimneys of the army huts.

'It's a lie! That's all it is—a thunderin' lie!' said a

1

private, loudly. His smooth face was flushed and his hands were thrust deep into his trousers' pockets. He took the matter as a personal insult. 'I don't believe this darned old army is ever going to move! We're stuck. I've got ready to move eight times in the last two weeks, and we **ain't** moved yet!'

The tall soldier who had introduced the rumour felt called upon to defend it. He and the loud one came near to blows over it. A corporal began to swear before them all. He had just lately put some new floor boards in his hut. In the spring he had felt that the army might march at any moment, but lately he had felt that they were all in a sort of eternal camp. Now, what was the truth of the matter?

Meanwhile, the tall soldier **bustled about** in importance. He was assailed on all sides:

'What's up, Jim?'

'The army's going to move.'

'What are you talking about—how do you know it is? Where?'

'Well, you can believe me or not, just as you like. I don't **care a hang**. You can take it or leave it—suit yourselves.'

There was a youthful private who had been listening with eager ears to the words of the tall soldier, and the varied comments of his comrades. After a while, he crawled through the hole that served as a door to his hut. He wanted to be alone with some new thoughts that had come to him.

He lay down on a wide bunk that stretched across the end of the room. At the other end, empty ammunition boxes served as furniture. They were grouped round the fireplace. Pictures from old illustrated weeklies were stuck on the wooden shelves, and three rifles were laid flat on pegs that had been driven into the wall. Soldiers' kit hung on handy nails and a folded tent was serving as part of the roof.

The youth lay in a little mood of surprise—so they were really going to fight at last? Even tomorrow, perhaps, there would be a real battle and he would be in it!

He had, of course, dreamed of battles all his life—vague conflicts in which he had seen himself in many struggles. But the time of real wars had long since gone—they were but dreams of old castles and daring deeds that had disappeared for ever.

At home his youthful eyes had looked upon this local war in his own country with distrust. It must be some sort of a play affair. Men were better now, more timid, and a better education had altered the old fighting instinct and held the passions in check.

Several times he had wanted to enlist. Tales of great events shook the country. He had read of marches, sieges, conflicts that had coloured his mind with extravagant pictures.

But his mother has discouraged him. She tried to pour cold water on his **patriotism**. She would calmly sit herself down and give him hundreds of reasons why he was so much more important on the farm than on the field of battle.

At last, however, he had rebelled against this **checking of his ambitions**. The newspapers, the gossip of the village, his own imagination of the excitement of battle won the day. One night he had gone to his mother's room and said, 'Ma, I'm going to enlist.'

'Henry, now don't you be a fool!' his mother replied, and then covered her face with her blanket. That was the end of the matter for that night.

Nevertheless, the next morning he had gone to a town that was near his mother's farm, and he had enlisted in a company that was forming there of local men.

When he returned, his mother was milking a **brindle** cow. Four other cows stood waiting. 'Ma, I've enlisted,' he said to her quietly. There was a short silence.

'The Lord's will be done, Henry,' his mother finally replied. She then continued to milk the brindle cow.

Later, when he had stood in the doorway in his soldier's uniform, with the light of excitement almost defeating his regrets at leaving home, he had seen two tears on his mother's wrinkled cheeks. But she had said nothing about returning with his shield, or 'on it', as the Greeks had said in the old days, and this rather disappointed him. He had prepared himself for a touching farewell scene, but her words in the end had destroyed all that.

She gave him plenty of practical advice as she peeled the potatoes:

'You watch out, Henry, and take good care of yourself in this fighting business. Don't go thinking you can **lick** the whole rebel army by yourself. You're just one little feller amongst a whole lot of others, and you've got to keep quiet and do what they tell you.

'I've knit you eight pairs of socks, Henry, and I've put in all your best shirts, because I want my boy to be as warm and comfortable as anybody in the army. And don't forget to send the socks back for me to mend as soon as they've got holes in.

'And always be careful to choose your company, Henry. There's lots of bad men in the army who will like nothing better than to learn you to drink and

4

swear. I don't want you ever to do anything that you'd be 'shamed for me to know about—so you just think as if I am watching you all the time and I guess you'll be all right. And here's a little bible for you to take, and remember when you want any advice you'll always find wisdom in it, Henry.

'And you must remember your father, too, child. Remember he never touched a drop of **likker** in his life, and seldom even swore an oath. And if you have to be killed, don't think of anything else but to do what's right. Don't forget about the socks and shirts, child, and I've put in a cup of blackberry jam with your bundle, because you like that more than anything. So good-bye, Henry, and watch out, and be a good boy.'

He had of course been impatient under the ordeal of this speech, but it was what he had expected. He departed in vague relief when the time came.

Still, when he looked back from the gate and had seen his mother among the potato peelings, with her brown face stained with tears, he felt a little ashamed at leaving her like that.

From his home he had gone to say good-bye to his one-time schoolmates. For the whole afternoon they had **thronged** about him and some of his fellows in blue, and the wonder and admiration had been enough to make them swell with pride—in fact they had strutted about like peacocks.

A certain light-haired girl had made fun of his **martial** spirit, but there was another darker girl who had watched his departure as he walked down the avenue, from a window up above, and he often thought of her.

On the way to Washington his spirits had soared. The regiment was fed and cared for at station after station as the troop train passed through, and they all felt like heroes. There was coffee and bread, and cold meats, pickles and cheese. As Henry **basked** in the smiles of the girls and was patted and complimented on every side, he felt growing within him the strength to do mighty deeds of arms.

But then, after many journeyings, there had come months of **monotony** in camp. He had thought that real war was a series of death struggles, with short spells between for sleep and food. But in the field the army had done little but sit still, talk and try to keep warm.

So Henry had come to think of himself merely as part of a vast blue army exercise. He had to look after his own personal comfort, for no one else would. For recreation he could just twiddle his thumbs. Then he was drilled and drilled and reviewed, and drilled and drilled again, and reviewed again.

The only enemy he had seen were some pickets along the river bank. They were sun-tanned and fairly friendly, and sometimes used their guns. When re-proached for this they said they were sorry and that the guns had gone off without their permission. One night, when Henry was on guard duty, a picket talked to him across the stream. He was a ragged-looking man and seemed quite friendly as they talked.

'Yank,' he had said to Henry, 'You're a right damn good feller.' This made Henry temporarily regret that there was a war.

There were many veterans' tales, and recruits were their prey. The older soldiers talked much of smoke, fire, blood, and of how their enemies would charge through hell's fire and brimstone to get hold of a **haversack**.

But Henry perceived that it didn't much matter what kind of soldiers he was going to fight, so long as they *fought*. He had a more important problem—when it came to real battle, would he indeed run from it? His vision of valour and glory began to seem to be made of impossible pictures.

As he thought about it all, he sprang from the bunk and began to pace nervously to and fro.

'Good Lord—what's the matter with me?' He knew he was really an **unknown quantity**—he would have to keep a tight hold upon himself, so that nothing he did might disgrace him. 'Good Lord!' he repeated in dismay. What sort of a soldier was he going to be?

After a time the tall soldier slid through the door hole. The loud private followed. They were still arguing.

'You can believe me or not,' he was saying as he entered. 'All you got to do is to sit down and wait, and pretty soon you'll find I was right.'

His comrade grunted. Then he said, 'Well, you don't know everything in the world, do you?'

'I didn't say I did,' replied the other, sharply. He began to pack various articles into his knapsack.

Henry stopped in his pacing and looked at what was being packed. 'Going to be a battle, sure, is there, Jim?'

'Of course there is,' replied the tall soldier. 'Of course there is. You just wait until tomorrow and you'll see one of the biggest battles that ever was. You just wait!'

'Thunder!' said Henry.

'Oh, you'll see fighting this time, my boy. Regular out-and-out fighting,' added Jim, with the air of a man who is about to exhibit a special battle for his friends.

'Huh!' grunted the loud one from his corner.

'Well,' Henry said, 'maybe this story will turn out

just like the others did and nothing will happen!'

'Not much it won't!' replied Jim, **exasperated**. 'Didn't the cavalry start off this morning? They say there's hardly any cavalry left in the camp. They're going to **Richmond**, or some place, while we fight the **Johnies**. The regiment's got the orders—it's all over the camp; anyone can see that.'

'Shucks!' said the loud one.

Henry had been silent, but now he said, 'Jim, tell me, how do you think the regiment will do, really?'

'Oh, they'll do all right, I guess, once they've got into it,' was the answer. 'There's been a lot of fun made of them, because they're new, of course, and all that, but I guess they'll fight all right, you'll see.'

'D'you think any of the boys will run?' persisted Henry.

'Oh, there may be a few of them run, but there's that kind in every regiment, specially when they first goes under fire,' said Jim, in a tolerant way. 'Of course it might happen the whole lot might start to run. Of course. But then again they might stand and fight like mad—you can't bet on nothing. It ain't likely they'll lick the whole rebel army in one go, but I reckon they'll fight better than some, if worse than others. That's the way I figger it. They call this regiment "Fresh Fish" and all that, but the boys come of good stock, and most of them'll fight like sin once they start shooting.' There was a strong emphasis on the last four words as he spoke.

'Oh, you think you know it all . . . . . ' began the loud soldier with scorn. The other turned savagely upon him and they began to shout at each other.

At last Henry interrupted them. 'Did you ever think you might run yourself, Jim?' he asked, laughing a little as if it was a bit of a joke. The loud soldier also giggled.

Jim waved his hand. 'Well, if a whole lot of the boys started to run, why, I've thought that it might get a bit too hot for Jim Conklin—and I suppose I might start to run, too, and if I once started, I'd run like the devil and no mistake. But if everyone was standing firm and fighting, why, sure I'd stand and fight with 'em—By Jiminey, I would, and I'll bet on that.'

Henry was glad to hear all this, and he felt grateful to Jim for it. He had feared that all of the untried men like themselves were full of a great and complete confidence. Now he felt a bit better about it.

Chapter 2

The next morning Henry found that Jim was quite mistaken about the regiment being under orders to move. Those, who yesterday had believed it now made fun of Jim, and those who had never believed it sneered at him. There was even a fight in which Jim severely beat up another soldier.

Henry felt, however, that all this did nothing to solve his problem; in fact it made it worse. The rumour had caused him increased concern for himself. With his questions unanswered, he felt once again that he was just a part of a blue army exercise.

After days of thinking he concluded that the only way to prove himself was to go into the firing line and see which way his legs would carry him. Unless he could face fire, blood and danger he would never know the answer to his problem; and so he began to long for the opportunity.

Meanwhile he tried to compare himself with his comrades. Jim, for one, he found reassuring. He had known him since childhood and he had always seemed unconcerned and supremely confident in himself, whatever happened. Surely, Henry thought, he himself could be the same? But then, perhaps Jim was over-confident about himself, or he might be a man of peace and obscurity in peace-time, but the sort who would shine in the reality of war.

If only Henry could have found someone who was as unsure of himself as he was! A sympathetic comparison of feelings would have been a joy, and a great help to him.

Occasionally he tried to **sound out** a comrade with searching questions. He was always on the look-out for men in the right mood to be questioned. But he never succeeded in making anyone confess to such doubts as he himself felt. At the same time he was afraid to confess his own doubts and fears openly. That would risk someone **sharing his confidence**, only to betray him later and make fun of him.

He could never make up his mind about his comrades; it depended on what mood he was in. Sometimes he believed them all to be heroes. Many of them he had known throughout their boyhood and he could picture them as being **instinctively** brave. Then, at other times, he realised that he might be mistaken in his judgment, and assured himself that they were privately as unsure of themselves as he was, if only they admitted it.

In his anxiety he continually complained at the inexcusable slowness of the generals. They seemed to him to be content to sit quietly on the river bank, and leave him bowed down by the weight of his problems. He wanted it all settled immediately. He could not bear it any longer, he said, and in his anger against the commanders he went about the camp grumbling like an old soldier.

One morning, however, he found himself in the ranks of a regiment that seemed to be preparing for battle. Men were whispering and repeating old rumours. In the dim light before daybreak their uniforms glowed purple. From across the river in the distance, the camp fires of the enemy still glowed, like red eyes. Against the eastern sky could be seen the figure of the colonel on a horse, appearing gigantic against the yellowing sky, as it stood on their side of the river.

Far away through the semi-darkness Henry could occasionally see dark shadows and hear the trampling of feet. But as a whole the regiment stood at rest and he grew increasingly impatient. He wondered how long they were to be kept waiting. He looked towards the colonel and saw him lift a gigantic arm and calmly stroke his moustache.

At last he heard the clatter of a horse's galloping hoofs. Henry thought it must be the coming of orders. Presently a horsemen **drew rein** before the colonel of the regiment; the two held a short conversation. The men in the front ranks craned their necks to watch and listen.

As the horseman galloped away, he turned to shout

over his shoulder, 'Don't forget that box of cigars!' The colonel mumbled something in reply. Henry wondered what a box of cigars had to do with war.

A moment later the regiment marched off in two columns into the darkness. It looked like a pair of monstrous serpents moving over the ground. There was an occasional flash and glimmer of steel from the back of the huge crawling monsters, and from the road could be heard creakings and grumblings, as men dragged their heavy guns along the way.

The men stumbled along, still guessing as to where they were going. Once a man fell down, and as he reached for his rifle a comrade accidentally trod upon his hand. The man who had fallen swore bitterly, but his fellows couldn't help laughing at his misfortune.

Dawn had now broken and the sun's rays at last struck full upon the earth. Henry saw that the landscape was streaked with two long, thin black columns which disappeared over the brow of a hill in front, and vanished to the rear in a wood.

The river was no longer in view. Jim boasted of his being proved right. 'I told you so, didn't I?' he exclaimed. Some of his companions told him that they, too, had expected this to happen, and congratulated themselves. But others maintained that Jim's ideas were not the right ones, and there continued to be much discussion and argument.

Henry took no part in this. He was too busy with his own unending problem. He studied the faces of his companions, ever on the watch to detect a fellow with like doubts and fears. He was disappointed. The men began to speak of a victory they seemed sure would be theirs; and Jim became increasingly confident. He was certain they were going to come around in behind the enemy. Everyone felt sorry for that part of the army which had been left behind on the river bank, robbed of the chance to be part of the victorious side.

Only Henry felt differently from all the others. Throughout the company there was much merriment. The loud-voiced soldier had everyone around him in fits of laughter at his sarcastic jokes at Jim's expense, and it was not long before all the men seemed to forget their mission.

While the regiment stood at rest by the roadside, a rather fat soldier tried to steal a horse from a farmyard. He was escaping with his prize when a young girl rushed from the farmhouse and grabbed the animal's mane. She argued fiercely with the soldier and stood her ground, with her eyes flashing and her cheeks flushed with anger. The soldiers looking on took her part, and became so interested in the dispute that they forgot their own larger war. They jeered at the thieving soldier and gave bold advice to the girl: 'Hit him with a stick,' they cried, and when the soldier retreated without the horse, the regiment rejoiced at his defeat and shouted congratulations to the girl. She stood panting, and regarded them all with defiance.

At nightfall the regiment halted and went into the fields to camp. Tents sprang up like strange plants, and camp fires, like peculiar red flowers, dotted the night.

Henry kept apart from his companions as much as he could and wandered some distance away. He lay down in the grass, and in the stillness of the night began to feel very sorry for himself. He wished he was at home again, making the endless rounds from the house to the barn, from the barn to the fields, and back to the house. He would sacrifice all the brass buttons in the army to be back again with the brindle cow and her mates. He told himself he was not cut out to be a soldier, and he thought how different he was from those men who were moving about round the camp fires.

As he lay thinking, he heard a rustle of grass, and turning his head, saw the loud soldier. He called out, 'Oh, Wilson!'

The latter approached and looked down at him. 'Why, hello, Henry: Is it you? What are you doing here?'

'Oh, just thinking,' said Henry.

Wilson sat down and carefully lit his pipe. 'You're getting blue, my boy. You're looking **thunderin' peeked**. What the dickens is wrong with you?'

'Oh, nothing,' said Henry.

Wilson then began to talk about the expected battle. 'Oh, we've got 'em now!' As he spoke his boyish face lit up with a cheerful smile, and his voice had a boastful ring to it. 'We've got 'em now. At last, by thunder, we'll lick 'em good!'

'If the truth was known,' he added, more soberly, 'up to now *they've* licked us pretty well every time. But this time—this time—we'll lick 'em good.'

'I thought you were objecting to this march a little while ago,' said Henry coldly.

'Oh, it wasn't that,' explained the other. 'I don't mind marching, if there's going to be fighting at the end of it. What I hate is this getting moved here and moved there, with no good coming of it, as far as I can see, except sore feet and damned **short rations**.'

'Well,' said Henry, 'Jim Conklin says we'll get plenty of fighting this time.'

'He's right, for once, I guess, though I can't see how he knew it. This time we're in for a big battle, and we've got the best end of it. That's for sure. Gee! How we'll **thump** 'em!'

He got up and began to pace to and fro excitedly. His enthusiasm made him walk with a lively step. He was fiery in his belief in success. He looked to the future with a clear, proud eye, and he swore with the air of an old soldier.

Henry watched him for a moment in silence. When he finally spoke, it was with bitterness. 'Oh, you're going to do great things, I suppose!'

Wilson blew a puff of smoke from his pipe. 'Oh, I don't know. I suppose I'll do as well as the rest. I'm going to try like thunder.'

'How do you know you won't run when the time comes?' asked Henry.

'Run?' said Wilson. 'Run?—of course not!' And he laughed aloud.

'Well,' continued Henry, 'lots of good enough men have thought they were going to do great things before a fight, but when the time came, they **skedaddled**.'

'Oh, that's all true, I guess,' replied Wilson, 'but I'm not going to skedaddle. The man that bets on my running will lose his money, that's all.'

'Oh, shucks!' said Henry. 'You ain't the bravest man in the world, are you?'

'No, I ain't,' exclaimed Wilson, 'and I didn't say I was. I said I was going to do my share of the fighting. That's what I said. And I am, too. Who do you think you are anyway? You talk as if you thought you was Napoleon Bonaparte.' He glared at Henry for a moment, and then strode away.

Henry called after him, 'Well, you needn't get mad about it!' But the other continued on his way and made no reply.

Now Henry felt more alone than ever. His failure to discover any resemblance in their points of view made him even more miserable. No one else seemed to have such a terrific personal problem. He was an outcast, alone in his doubts and fears.

He went slowly to his tent and lay down on a blanket beside the tall figure of Jim, now fast asleep and snoring. In the darkness he imagined that he might flee in fear, while others were coolly going about their country's business.

As he sweated with the pain of his thoughts, he heard the low voices of some men playing cards. 'I'll bid five.' 'Make it six.' 'Seven.' 'Seven goes.'

He stared at the red, flickering reflection of a fire on the white canvas wall of his tent until, exhausted and feeling quite ill from the pain of his suffering, he fell asleep.

Chapter 3

When the next night came, the columns filed across two **pontoon bridges** over the river. A glowing fire behind them lit the waters under the bridges with sudden gleams of silver or gold. Behind the far shore a range of hills curved against the sky. Insects sang in the night air.

After this crossing, Henry felt that at any moment he might be suddenly shot at out of the dark woods. He kept his eyes watchfully on the darkness ahead.

But his regiment got to its next camping place, and the men slept the brave sleep of tired men. In the morning they were woken early and hurried along a narrow road that led deep into the forest. It was during this rapid march that the regiment began to lose many of the signs of a newly-formed unit and to settle into some sort of routine.

The men had begun to count the miles and grow tired. Grumblings increased. 'Tired feet and short rations!' said the loud soldier. 'I told you how it would be.'

After a time they began to lighten their loads. Some tossed their knapsacks aside, some hid them carefully, saying they would return for them later. Men got out of their thick shirts. Soon very few of them carried anything but their necessary clothing, blankets, haversacks, water bottles, arms and ammunition.

'You can eat, drink, sleep and shoot,' said Jim to Henry. 'That's really all you need. What do you want to carry—a hotel?'

Gradually the regiment, relieved of some of its burdens, began to move faster. But there was loss of some valuable knapsacks and many a good shirt.

But the regiment did not look like a veteran army yet. There wasn't enough variety in the hats. The hats of a regiment on the march should represent the history of its headgear for a number of years. And there were no letters of faded gold upon their colours; no battle honours. The flag was new and beautiful and the **standard-bearer** oiled the pole regularly.

Presently the army again sat down to think. The smell of the pine trees was in the men's nostrils. The sound of axe blows rang through the distant part of the forest, and the insects seemed to **croon** like old women. Henry thought it was all like the usual army exercise.

One gray dawn, however, he was roused early by Jim and he found himself running down a woodland road before he was properly awake. His water bottle flapped against his thigh and his haversack bobbed at his back. His musket bounced from his shoulder at each stride and his cap was not properly on.

He could hear the men whispering. 'What's it all about? Why are we in such a hurry? Billy, keep off my feet, you run like a cow! Where the devil are we running to?'

From the distance came the sudden spatter of shots. He was bewildered. He tried to think, but all he knew was that if he fell down, those behind would trample on him. He was being carried along by the mob.

The sun's rays gained strength and he could see more and more men come into view. He could not escape from the regiment. It enclosed him with its rules and tradition like a box.

It occurred to him that he had never really wished to come to the war. Had he really enlisted of his own free will? He had been dragged by a cruel government, and now they were taking him along to be slaughtered. The regiment slid down a bank and waded across a stream. The current moved slowly along, and from the black water it seemed as if white bubble eyes looked at the men as they moved through it.

As they climbed the hill on the farther side, the artillery began to boom. Henry scrambled up the bank at speed, curious to see if there would be a scene of battle revealed. But instead all he could see ahead were little fields and trees. Spread over the fields he could see men running here and there and firing at the landscape. There seemed to be a battle line on a clearing that lay in the sunlight. A flag fluttered.

Other regiments scrambled up the bank. The brigade was formed into a line of battle, and after a pause moved slowly through the woods behind the groups of **skirmishers**.

Henry tried to observe everything—taking no notice of the prickly branches or the stones around his feet. It seemed to him a wrong place for a battle field. The shots of the skirmishers ahead of him rang in the distance. The landscape seemed to threaten him.

Once they came upon a dead soldier. He lay upon his back, staring at the sky. He was dressed in an unfamiliar suit of faded grey. Henry could see that the soles of his shoes had been worn to the thinness of writing paper, and a dead foot projected from one of them. It seemed as if fate had revealed to his enemies the poverty which he had hidden from his friends when he was alive.

The ranks of men avoided the corpse. The dead man lay quite alone. Henry looked keenly at the white face as the wind raised the tawny beard. He felt he wanted to walk round and round the body and stare. It was the impulse of the living to try to read in dead eyes the answer to every question. To Henry it was *The Question*.

During the march Henry felt his keeness fade to nothing. His curiosity was now satisfied. If an intense battle scene had caught his attention as he came to the top of the bank, he might have gone roaring on, but this advance upon Nature's woods and fields was too calm and uneventful.

A house standing quietly in distant fields looked mysterious. The shadows in the woods seemed to threaten. He thought that the generals did not know what they were doing. It was all a trap. Rifles could burst out of the forests at any moment—brigades of iron could appear from the rear. The enemy would soon swallow the whole army. He stared about him, expecting to see death approaching.

Henry thought he must break ranks and warn his comrades. They must not all be killed like pigs, and he was sure that that was what would happen if they were not told of all the dangers. The generals were idiots to send them all marching like this into a trap. There was only one pair of eyes in the brigade and those were his. He would step out and make a speech.

But the line went calmly on through fields and woods. Henry looked at the men nearest him and saw expressions of deep interest, as if they were studying something. One or two walked as if upon thin ice, but the greater part of the untested men appeared quiet and absorbed. They were going to look at war, the red animal—war, the blood-swollen god, and they were deeply involved in this march. Even if they were tottering with fear they would laugh at his warnings and jeer at his fears. He began to lag behind, with tragic glances at the sky.

Presently, he was surprised by the lieutenant of his company, who began to shout in a loud and insolent voice, and wave his sword at him: 'Come on, man, get up into line. No **skulking**'ll do here!' This made Henry hurry along, but he hated the lieutenant, who was obviously a mere brute with no appreciation of searching minds.

After a time the brigade was halted again in the cathedral light of a forest with its roof of spreading trees. The busy skirmishers were still running ahead, and through the aisles of the wood could be seen the floating smoke from their rifles.

During this halt many of the men began erecting small mounds in front of themselves for protection. They used stones, sticks, earth and anything that might turn a bullet. Some wished to fight standing upright, and said they scorned these devices, but others pointed to the veterans on the flanks of the line who were digging at the ground like terriers. In a short time there was quite a barricade along the regimental front, but it was not long afterwards before they were ordered to move on again.

'Well, then, what did they march us out here for?' Henry demanded of Jim Conklin. The latter began to explain with calm faith, although he had been compelled to leave a little **rampart** of stones and dirt to which he had devoted much care and attention.

When the regiment took up a fresh position another line of small entrenchments appeared. They ate their noon meal behind a third one. They were moved from this one also. They were marched from place to place with apparent aimlessness.

The ordeal of waiting became too much for Henry. He considered that the generals had no proper purpose.

21

He was in a fever of impatience. 'I can't stand this much longer,' he said to Jim. 'I don't see what good it does to make us wear out our legs for nothing.'

He wished to return to camp knowing that either this had been but an army exercise, or that he must go into battle and discover if he'd been a fool in his doubts and was in truth a man of courage.

Jim was making a sandwich of pork and hard biscuits, and proceeded to eat it, unconcerned. 'Oh, I suppose we must keep a watch on the country, to keep the rebels from getting too close, or to make them think we're on the move, or something.'

'Huh!' said Wilson.

'Well,' said Henry, 'I'd rather do anything than go on tramping round the country all day, doing no good to nobody and just tiring ourselves out.'

'So would I,' said Wilson. 'It ain't right. I tell you if anyone with any sense was running this army it . . .'

'Oh, shut up!' roared Jim. 'You little fool. You ain't had that coat and trousers on for six months, and yet you talk as if . . .'

'Well, I want to do some fighting anyway,' interrupted the other. 'I didn't come here to walk. I could have walked at home—round and round the barn, if I just wanted to walk.'

Jim swallowed another sandwich, red-faced, but as he chewed he seemed to commune with the food—he was always calm and contented when he was eating.

On the march, Jim went along with the stride of a hunter, objecting to neither pace nor distance; and he had not even raised his voice when he had been ordered away from three little piles of earth and stone, each of which had been an engineering feat worthy of being sacred to the name of his grandmother.

In the afternoon the regiment went out over the same ground it had covered in the morning. The landscape then ceased to threaten Henry. He had been close to it and become familiar with it.

When, however, they began to pass into a new region, Henry thought again about his problem. He thought perhaps it would be better to get killed early and end his troubles. Regarding death out of the corner of his eye, he thought that really it would be nothing but rest, and it seemed to him he had made too much fuss about it. He would die; he would go to some place where he would be understood. It was useless to expect understanding from such men as the lieutenant. Complete understanding would be in the grave.

The firing got louder and there was cheering in the distance. Henry could see men running and there were dangerous flashes of rifle fire. Clouds of smoke drifted slowly across the fields. The noise increased like the distant roar of an oncoming train.

A brigade ahead of them went into action and a long grey wall stretched ahead of it, until it took a second glance to make sure it was smoke.

Henry forgot his idea of getting killed, and gazed on the scene fascinated. His eyes were wide and his mouth open in amazement.

Suddenly he felt a heavy hand on his shoulder. He turned and saw that Wilson had come up to him. He was very pale and his lip was trembling as he spoke: 'It's my first and last battle, old boy,' he said sorrowfully. 'Something tells me . . . '

'What?' said Henry, astonished.

'It's my first and last battle, old boy,' repeated Wilson. 'I'm done for this time, and—I want you to take these things—to my folks.' He ended with a sob, as he handed Henry a little packet done up in a yellow envelope.

'Why, what the devil . . . ?' began Henry, but Wilson gave him a glance as if from the depths of a tomb, raised a limp hand as if in final farewell, and turned away.

Chapter 4

The brigade had been halted on the edge of a wood. The men crouched among the trees and pointed their guns towards the fields. They tried to look beyond the smoke. Out of the haze they could see men running. Some shouted information and gestured as they hurried.

The men of the new regiment watched and listened eagerly, while their tongues were busy with the gossip of the battle. They passed on rumours that had flown like birds out of the unknown.

'They say Perry has been driven back with big loss.'

'Yes, Carrott went to the hospital. He said he was sick. That smart lieutenant is commanding G Company in his place. The boys say they won't be under Carrott no more, even if they all have to desert. They always knew he was a . . .'

'The general, he says he's going to take command of the 304th when we go into action, and then he says we'll do such fighting as never another regiment done!'

'They say we're catching it over on the left. They say the enemy drove our line into a devil of a swamp and took Hannises' battery.'

'No such thing. Hannises' battery was along here a minute ago.'

'I met one of the 148th boys and he says his brigade fought the whole rebel army for four hours on the main road and killed about five thousand of 'em. He says one more such fight as that and the war'll be over!'

'Bill wasn't scared either. No sir! It wasn't that. Bill doesn't get scared easy. He was just mad when that fellow trod on his hand, way back. He said he was willing to give his hand for his country, but he was darned if he was going to have any darned rebel walking on it. So he went to the hospital and missed the fight. Three fingers were crushed. The darn doctor wanted to cut 'em off, but Bill, he raised the helluva row, I hear. Funny fellow, Bill.'

'Hear what the old colonel says, boys? He says he'll shoot the first man that'll turn and run.'

'He'd better try it. I'd like to see him shoot at *me*.'

'Ed Williams over in A Company, he says the rebels will all drop their guns and surrender if we once give 'em one good licking.'

'Oh, thunder, Ed Williams, what does he know? Ever since he got shot at **on picket** he's been running the war.'

'Hear the news, boys? Corkright's crushed the whole rebel right and captured two whole divisions. We'll be back in winter quarters sooner than we think!'

25

'I tell you I've been all over that there country where the rebel right is, and it's the nastiest part of their line. It's all hills and little damn **creeks**. I'll bet my shirt Corkright never shifted them down there.'

'Well, he's a fighter and if they could be licked, he'd lick 'em.'

The din of battle in front was now so tremendous that Henry and his comrades were shocked into silence. A shell screamed overhead as the reserves crouched down in a huddle. It landed in the wood, flinging up red-brown earth, and there was a little shower of pine needles. Bullets began to whistle among the branches. Twigs and leaves came sailing down. Many of the men were constantly dodging and ducking their heads.

The lieutenant of Henry's company was shot in the hand. He began to swear so colourfully, that some of the men laughed nervously. His swearing relieved the tension; it was as if he had hit his fingers with a hammer at home. He held his wounded hand carefully away from his side so that the blood would not drip upon his trousers. The captain of the company produced a handkerchief and began to bind the lieutenant's wound. There was an argument between them as to how it should be done.

Meanwhile the battle flag in the distance jerked about madly. The billowing smoke was filled with flashes of gun fire. Men running swiftly emerged from the smoke, and their numbers grew until it could be seen that the whole forward command was fleeing from the enemy. The flag suddenly sank down as if it was dying. It looked like a gesture of despair.

Wild cries came from behind the wall of smoke, and out of the grey cloud poured a moblike body of men who galloped like wild horses.

The veteran regiments on the right and left of the 304th, who were also being held in reserve, began to jeer. Mingled with the hiss of the bullets and the scream of the shells were insults and sarcastic advice about where to find safety.

But the new regiment was breathless with horror. 'Gawd! Our fellows up front got crushed!' whispered the man at Henry's elbow.

All in vain did their officers try to halt the fleeing throng, but they were carried along on the stream of men. They were cursing and striking about them with their swords and with their fists, punching every head they could reach. But in their rush the running men were apparently all deaf and blind.

Frequently, over all the noise, the jeering cries of the veterans could be heard, but the retreating men were not even aware of the presence of an audience.

The **stampede** seemed to resemble a floodlike force that could drag sticks, stones and men from the ground. But the reserves knew they had to hold on. Henry had one brief thought in the midst of all this **chaos**. He had not yet seen the monster that had caused the other troops to flee. He thought that if he did get a view of it, very likely he might run better than the rest of them.

Chapter 5

There were moments of waiting. They made Henry think of the village street at home, before the arrival of the circus parade.

He remembered how he had stood as a boy, thrilled with a desire to follow the lady on the white horse, or the band in its faded chariot. He saw the yellow road, the lines of expectant people, the plain houses. He particularly remembered an old fellow who used to sit upon a box in front of the shop and pour scorn on such parades.

Some one cried, 'Here they come!'

There was a rustling and muttering among the men. They displayed a feverish desire to have every possible cartridge ready to their hands. Jim, having prepared his rifle, produced a red handkerchief and began to knot it about his throat with great care, when up and down the line there came a great roar: 'Here they come! Here they come!'

Across the smoky fields came a grey swarm of enemy soldiers, charging towards them, yelling as they came. They ran, stooping and swinging their rifles at all angles. A flag waved in front of them, tilted forward. As Henry saw the men, he suddenly thought that perhaps he had not loaded his gun. He tried to remember, but he could not.

A hatless general pulled up his horse near the colonel of the 304th. He shook his fist in the other's face.

'You've got to hold 'em back!' he shouted, savagely. 'You've got to hold 'em back!'

The Colonel began to stammer in confusion. 'A . . . all right, General, all . . . right, by Gawd! We'll do . . . we'll do our best, General!'

The general galloped away with a passionate gesture.

The colonel began to swear and scold—he looked back at his men as if he resented their presence.

A man near Henry was mumbling to himself, 'Oh, we're in for it now! Oh, we're in for it now!'

The captain of the company ran to and fro at the rear, calling to his boys like a schoolmistress: 'Reserve your fire, boys. Don't shoot till I tell you—save your fire—wait till they get close—don't be damned fools!'

Sweat streamed down Henry's face. He frequently wiped his eyes with his coat sleeve. His mouth was half open. After one glance at the foes that swarmed in front of him, he threw his rifle into position and fired a wild shot. From then on he used it with automatic ease.

He suddenly lost all concern for himself. He became not a man but a member of something bigger than himself—a regiment, an army, a cause, or a country—he was joined in a common bond. For some time he felt he could no more move away from the others than a little finger can move itself from a hand.

The noise gave him assurance. The regiment was like a firework which, once lit, proceed to burst in its vitality until it is finished. And he was not alone. He was always conscious of his comrades about him. He felt the brotherhood of battle was more potent than the cause for which they fought. It was a mysterious **fraternity**, born of the smoke and the danger of death. They were all in it together.

Presently Henry began to feel the effects of the battle—a blistering sweat, a feeling that his eyeballs were about to crack like hot stones; a burning roar filled his ears.

There was a heated rage in the intent expression on

all their faces. Many of the men were making loud noises—snarls, curses, prayers—and Jim was swearing curious oaths in a loud voice. A man suddenly broke out, 'Hell, why don't they come and support us? Why don't they send support? Do they think . . . '

Men were surging and swaying in every possible attitude. Steel ramrods clanged with the endless noise of men reloading the hot rifle barrels. Cartridge boxes were unfastened, their flaps bobbing about with each movement. Rifles were jerked to the shoulder and fired without aim into the smoke where the enemy moved like puppets.

The officers ran to and fro roaring directions and encouragements. They shouted and howled at the men with all the strength of their lungs.

The lieutenant of Henry's company had seen a soldier run screaming from the volley of rifle fire. Behind the lines these two acted an isolated scene. The man was blubbering and staring at the lieutenant, who had seized him by the collar and was hitting him, until he drove him back into the ranks with stern words. The soldier still stared with animal-like eyes at the officer. Then he tried to reload his gun, but his shaking hands were helpless. The lieutenant was obliged to assist him.

Men began to drop here and there like bundles. The captain of the company had been killed in an earlier action. His body lay stretched out like a tired man resting, and on his face was an astonished and sorrowful look.

The blubbering man was grazed by a shot that made the blood stream down his face. He clapped both hands to his head and ran. Another grunted suddenly as if he had been struck with a club in the stomach. He sat down and gazed about him in a mute **reproach**. Further up the line a man behind a tree had his knee joint shattered by a bullet. At once he dropped his rifle and gripped the tree with both arms. There he remained, clinging desperately to the tree and crying for help.

At last a yell came from the long line of men, as the firing eased off for a while. As the smoke drifted away, Henry saw that the enemy had withdrawn into groups. He saw one of them climb to the top of a fence, straddle a rail and fire a last parting shot. Now the waves seemed to have receded, leaving dark debris on the ground.

Henry felt as if he would suffocate. He became aware of the foul air around him, thick with fumes and smoke. He was dirty and sweating, like a **stoker in a foundry**. He grasped his water bottle and took a long swallow of the warm water.

Up and down the line came voices of relief: 'Well, we held 'em back—we held 'em—darned if we didn't!' They grinned at each other; smiles on their grimy faces. Henry felt the joy of a man who at last has time to look about him and feel some satisfaction.

But underfoot there were a few motionless forms, twisted in fantastic shapes, with arms and legs turned in unnatural attitudes. They looked as if they had fallen from a great height.

From the rear came the sound of a battery, throwing shells over them. The flash of the guns startled Henry, and for a moment he thought they were aiming at him.

The guns **squatted** in a row like iron creatures, and their busy servants ran here and there as they worked swiftly to feed their iron masters. A small procession of wounded men were walking slowly towards the rear.

31

It was like a flow of blood from the torn body of the brigade.

To the right and to the left were the dark lines of other troops. They seemed to number thousands. In the distance Henry saw a tiny battery dashing along the line of the horizon, the tiny riders beating the tiny horses. From a sloping hill came the sound of cheerings and clashes. Smoke drifted slowly through the leaves.

Here and there were flags, the red of the stripes standing out, splashing warm colour upon the dark lines of men. Henry felt the old thrill at the sight of the flags. They were like beautiful birds, unafraid of the storm.

As he listened to the din that came from near and far, he realised that there was more fighting, over there and over there and over there. Before this he had thought that all the battle was directly under his nose.

As he gazed around him, Henry felt a glad astonishment at the blue, pure sky, and the gleam of the sun on the trees and fields. It was amazing that Nature had gone calmly on with her golden process in the midst of so much confusion.

Chapter 6

Next morning Henry awakened slowly. It took him some time to realise where he was and what he had been through. Then he picked up his cap, adjusted his jacket and relaced his boots. So it was over at last! He had passed the supreme test, and overcome the terrible challenge of war.

He felt very pleased with himself, and found it a delightful sensation. Thinking over that last battle scene, he thought that he must be a fine fellow to have fought so well. He had lived up to ideals which he had thought were beyond him.

He made cheerful remarks to his fellows. 'Gee, ain't it hot?' he said to one man who was wiping the sweat from his face with his coat sleeve. 'You bet!' said the other, giving Henry a friendly grin. 'I never saw such a darned heat. Gee, yes! And I hope we don't have no more fighting till a week from Monday.'

There were handshakes and chat with men whom Henry recognised, but whose names he did not know, and with whom he now felt the bonds of friendship. He helped one comrade bind up a wound on his shin.

Then, suddenly, there were cries of amazement around him; 'Here they come again! Here they come again!' Looking across the fields Henry saw that ever-increasing numbers of the enemy were pouring out of a wood in the distance. He could see again the tilted flag of the enemy speeding forward.

Shells began screaming overhead again and exploded in the grass or amongst the trees. The men groaned, and their disappointment showed on their grimy faces. Their stiff bodies moved slowly and they felt rebellious at the harsh task once again imposed on them, as they watched the headlong approach of the enemy.

They complained to each other: 'Oh, say, this is too much of a good thing! Why can't someone send us reinforcements?'

'We ain't never going to stand this second banging. I didn't come here to fight the whole rebel army!'

There was one man who exclaimed, 'I wish Bill Smithers had trod on my hand, instead of me treading on his.'

Henry stared. Surely, he thought, this was impossible. He waited as if he expected the enemy to stop, apologise, and retire bowing. It must be a mistake.

But the firing began somewhere on the regimental line, and ripped along in both directions. Great clouds of smoke developed out of the level sheets of flame spouting from the rifles. The flag was sometimes lost in this mass of vapour, but more often it could be seen held high, shining in the sun.

Henry's eyes had the look of a frightened horse. The muscles of his neck strained, and the muscles of his arms felt numb. His hands felt large and awkward, and his knees began to feel weak and uncertain.

The words of his comrades before the firing began came back to him: 'Oh, say, this is too much of a good thing! What do they take us for—why don't they send reinforcements? I didn't come to fight the whole rebel army.'

He began to exaggerate the **endurance**, the skill, and the courage of the enemy who were charging towards them. He was astonished at their **perseverance**. They must be made of steel. It was a hopeless prospect to have to fight against such odds, perhaps even until sundown.

He slowly lifted his rifle, and blazed away at a

cluster of men in the midst of the field. Then he stopped to see, as best he could through the smoke, what the effect had been. All he could see was that the ground was still covered with men running towards him, yelling. It seemed to him like an attack by **irresistible** dragons. He felt as if he had lost the use of his legs, and waited, with his eyes shut, expecting any moment to be gobbled up.

A man near to him, who up to this moment had been working away feverishly at his rifle, suddenly stopped and ran away howling. To Henry, it was a revelation that one who had seemed to be setting an example of great courage, should be so suddenly filled with fear. It was as if he had come to the edge of a cliff at midnight and was suddenly aware of the danger. He, too, threw down his rifle and fled. He did not feel ashamed; he just ran like a rabbit.

A few others began to run away through the smoke. Henry turned his head and saw these few forms. He yelled with fright and swung around. For a moment, he lost all sense of direction; he seemed to be threatened from all directions.

He began to speed towards the rear as fast as he could. His rifle and cap were gone. His unbuttoned coat bulged in the wind. The flap of his cartridge box bobbed wildly, and his water bottle swung behind on its slender cord. On his face was all the horror of those things which he imagined.

The lieutenant sprang forward shouting at him. His face was flushed with anger as he thrust at Henry with his sword. But Henry ran on like a blind man. Two or three times he fell down, and once he knocked his shoulder so heavily against a tree that he fell headlong on the ground.

Since he had turned his back on the fight his fears had greatly increased. As he ran on he mingled with others. There were men on his right and on his left, and he heard footsteps behind him. He thought that all the regiment was fleeing. In his flight the sound of following footsteps gave him some sense of relief, for he felt that death from the pursuers would strike first at those behind him. So he ran like a crazed sprinter in his desire to keep them in the rear. It became a race with death.

As he went across a small field, he found himself in an area where shells were falling. They hurtled over his head with long wild screams. Once, one blew up before him, and the vivid lightning of the explosion barred the way in which he wanted to go. He fell to the ground and then, springing up again, dashed off through some bushes.

He came within sight of a battery in action, and was both thrilled and amazed by it. The men there seemed to be unaware that they would soon be wiped out. They were engaging a distant hostile battery, and seemed lost in admiration of their own shooting. They were continually bending over their guns, as if they were patting them on the back and encouraging them with words. Henry pitied them as he ran. Idiots! Machine-like fools! What was the use of planting shells in the midst of the other battery formation, when the enemy infantry were swooping out of the woods? Yet, somehow he felt pity for the guns, standing in a row like six good, bold comrades.

He saw a brigade going to the relief of its fellows. He scrambled up a small hill to get a better view of it, and was impressed by the way it kept its formation on difficult ground. The blue of the line was edged with steel, and the brilliant flags showed up clearly. Officers were shouting orders. The sight filled Henry with wonder. The brigade was hurrying to be swallowed by the infernal mouth of the war god. What manner of men were they, anyhow? Ah, they were of some wondrous breed! Or else they did not understand. The fools!

Henry went on, and as the noise became less, slowed his pace a little. Presently, he came upon a general seated on a horse that pricked its ears in an interested way at the battle. The leather of its saddle and bridle gleamed brightly, but the quiet man astride the horse looked drab upon such a splendid animal. Staff officers were galloping hither and thither, so that sometimes the general was surrounded by horsemen, and at other times he was quite alone. He appeared very concerned, like a business man worrying about his balance sheet.

Henry went as near as he dared, hoping to overhear something of what was said. Perhaps, even, the general, unable to understand what was really happening, might call upon him for information. And he could tell him a thing or two! He knew everything. The force was surely in a fix, and any fool could see that if they did not retreat while they had the opportunity—why . . .

He felt he would like to strike the general, or at least approach him and tell him plainly what he thought of him. It was criminal to stay calmly in one spot and make no effort to halt the destruction. If only the general would ask him for news!

As he hung about, he heard the general call out irritably: 'Tompkins, go over and see Taylor, and tell him not to be in such a hurry: tell him to halt his brigade on the edge of the wood: tell him to detach a regiment—say I think the centre will break if we don't help it out: tell him to hurry up.'

A slim young officer on a fine **chestnut** horse caught these words from the mouth of the general. He soon made his horse leap into a gallop in his haste to go upon his mission, leaving a cloud of dust behind him.

A moment later, Henry saw the general bounce excitedly in his saddle. 'By heaven, they've held 'em!' The general leaned forward, his face lit up with excitement. 'Yes, by heaven, they've held 'em. They've held 'em!'

He began to roar at his staff: 'We'll **wallop** 'em now. We'll wallop 'em now. We've got 'em, sure!' He turned suddenly to an aide: 'Here—you—Jones—quick—ride after Tompkins—see Taylor—tell him to go in—keep at it—like blazes—anything!'

As another officer **spurred** his horse after the first messenger, the general beamed on those round him like a sun. He kept repeating: 'By heaven, they've held 'em.' His excitement made his horse rear, and he merrily kicked and swore at it. He seemed to be doing a little dance of joy on horseback.

Chapter 7

Henry cringed as if discovered in a crime. By heavens, they had won after all! The stupid line had remained firm and become victors. He could hear cheering. He lifted himself upon his toes and looked in the direction of the fight. From beneath the smoke came the clatter of musketry. Hoarse cries told of an advance. He turned away, amazed and angry.

Henry thought that he had been wronged. He had fled because he must save himself—a little piece of the army. He thought it was the duty of everyone to save himself if possible. Later the officers could fit all the little pieces together again and remake the battle front. After all, if none of the men were wise enough to save themselves from death at such a time—where would be the army? He himself had been wise and full of common sense.

He thought of his comrades. The blue line had withstood the attack and won. But he was bitter over it. The blind ignorance and stupidity of the little pieces had betrayed him. He had seen their lack of sense in holding the line when intelligent thought would have shown them that it was impossible. He had fled because of his superior knowledge. He could prove that they had been fools.

He wondered what they would all say when he appeared in camp later. He heard in his mind their howls of scorn. They would never understand his wiser point of view.

He began to pity himself. He staggered along with his head down and a great despair in his mind. In his eyes there was the expression of a criminal who knows he is guilty, but cannot find words to explain what

39

good reasons he had. To get away from the firing he went into the thicker woods where he could hide.

He had to force his way through creepers, bushes and brambles, and he dreaded that the noise he made might bring men to look at him. So he went further, seeking dark and hidden places.

After a time the sun blazed away among the trees. The insects made rhythmical noises. A woodpecker poked his bright head around the side of a tree, and a bird flew swiftly by. The rumble of death had gone. Nature reigned in the woods with no ears, and its religion of peace gave him comfort. He thought of Nature as a woman who has a deep dislike of pain and suffering.

Henry threw a pine cone at a chattering squirrel, and the tiny animal ran up into a tree-top and looked cheekily down at him. This was Nature's law, he felt— the instinct to recognise danger and run from it. No squirrel would stand stolidly baring its furry belly to attack, and die with a glance up to heaven for approval. On the contrary, this one had fled as fast as its legs could carry it. Nature was of Henry's mind; she was on his side.

Soon he reached a place where the arching branches made a sort of chapel. Pine needles made a gentle brown carpet. There was a religious half-light. He entered, pushing the green doors aside. Then he stopped, horror stricken.

He was being looked at by a dead man who sat with his back against a tree. The corpse was dressed in a uniform that once had been blue, but was now faded to a gloomy shade of green. The eyes, staring at Henry, had changed to the dull hue to be seen on the side of a dead fish. The mouth was open. Its red had changed to a dreadful yellow. Over the grey skin of the face ran little black ants, to and fro and across the lips.

Henry was turned to stone before this sight. He remained staring into the liquid-looking eyes. The dead man and the living man exchanged a long look. Then the youth put one hand behind himself and held on to a branch. Leaning upon this he retreated, step by step, with his face still set towards the corpse. He feared that if he turned his back the body might spring up and pursue him.

His unguided feet caught in the brambles below, and the branches round him threatened to throw him over. He felt a faint urge to touch the body, then shuddered in disgust. At last he fled, not **heeding** the clinging brambles. He could still see in his mind the black ants swarming on the grey face, and crawling near the eyes.

After a time, he paused, breathless and panting, back in the main part of the wood. He imagined some strange voice might come from the dead throat and call after him with threats.

The trees round the doorway of the chapel moved gently in the soft wind. A sad silence closed upon the little **sanctuary**.

Chapter 8

The trees began softly to sing an evening hymn. The sun sank in the sky until its reddish rays struck the forest. The noises of the insects ceased as if they had folded their wings in prayer. There was silence, except for the sighing of the trees in the wind.

Then, suddenly, upon this stillness there broke an almighty crash of sound. It was the roar of guns and the crack of rifles in the distance.

Henry was **awestruck**. His mind was confused by the **medley** of noises, and he pictured the two armies at each other like beasts of the jungle. For a time he just listened. Then he began to run in the direction of the battle.

He realised that it was strange for him to be running in this way towards that which he had been at such pains to avoid. It was as if he was thinking that, if two heavenly bodies were about to clash, many would wish to get up on the roof tops to watch the collision.

As he ran, he became aware that the noises of the forest had ceased. The trees were hushed and stood motionless. The thunderous noise of the battle was ear-splitting.

It suddenly came into Henry's mind that the fight in which he had taken part was as nothing compared with the present clash of men and guns. This uproar suggested a battle of the gods. By comparison, the engagement from which he and some of his fellows had fled seemed unimportant. He even thought it slightly humorous, for they had taken it all very seriously, even thinking that they were deciding the war.

He went rapidly on. He wanted to get to the edge of the forest, so that he might peer out and watch this great encounter. Sometimes the brambles formed chains and tried to hold him back. Trees stretched out their arms and forbade him to pass. But he obstinately took roundabout ways and presently came to an opening, from where he could see long grey walls of smoke along which lay the lines of battle. The booming of the guns shook the earth, and his ears hurt with the noise of constant rifle fire.

He was stunned, and stood still for a moment, gazing in shock at the sight which greeted him. But soon he felt compelled to move forward again. The battle was like the grinding of an immense and terrible machine. Its grim powers and workings fascinated him. He must go close and see this machine produce corpses.

He came to a fence and climbed over it. On the other side the ground was littered with discarded clothes and abandoned rifles. A dead soldier lay stretched out with his face hidden in his arms. Further off was a group of four or five corpses lying in the evening sun.

Henry felt that he was an intruder. This part of the battle ground belonged to the dead men, and he hurried away, vaguely fearful that one of the swollen corpses would rise and tell him to be gone.

He came finally to a road, from which he could see in the distance, partly screened by a smoke haze, a body of troops. Away from them, and down the road towards him, a blood-stained crowd streamed towards the rear, cursing, groaning and wailing. But above the cries of anguish could be heard the sound of the artillery and rifle fire, and the cheering of those still sustaining the fight. Out of all this noise, then, came the steady stream of the wounded.

One of the wounded men had a shoeful of blood. He

hopped like a schoolboy in a game, and was alternately laughing and crying, hysterically. Another was swearing that he had been shot in the arm through the commanding general's mismanagement of the army. A third man was marching with the air of a drum major. On his face was an awful mixture of merriment and pain. As he marched he sang in a high, shaky voice:

> 'Sing a song of victory
> A pocket full of rye,
> Five and twenty dead men
> Baked in a pie.'

Parts of the procession limped and staggered to the tune he sang. A fourth man, the most striking of all, had the grey seal of death already upon his face. His lips were curled in hard lines and his teeth were clenched. His hands were bloody from where he had pressed them upon his wound. He seemed to be awaiting the moment when he would pitch forward and fall headlong to the ground. He tramped like the ghost of a soldier, his eyes burning, staring into the unknown.

An officer was carried along by two privates. He was irritable. 'Don't joggle so, Johnson, you fool,' he cried. 'Think my leg is made of iron? If you can't carry me properly, put me down and let someone else do it.' He shouted at the tottering crowd of wounded who blocked the way of his bearers. 'Say, make way there, can't you? Make way.' The men **sulkily** gave way and kept to the sides of the road. As he was carried past, they made insolent remarks, and when he raged in reply and threatened them, they told him to be damned.

The shoulder of one of the bearers knocked heavily

against the ghost-like soldier, who was staring into the unknown.

Henry joined this crowd of wounded men and marched along with them. Their torn bodies bore witness to the awful engines of death with which they had been caught.

Messengers on horseback occasionally broke through the crowd in the roadway, scattering wounded men right and left. As they galloped on, they were followed by jeers and howls. The pitiful procession was not only disturbed by the messengers, but also, sometimes, by batteries of artillery that came swinging and thumping down upon them, the officers shouting orders to clear the way.

There was a **tattered** man, fouled with dust, blood and gunpowder stains from head to foot, who trudged along quietly by Henry's side. He was listening intently to the lurid tales of a bearded sergeant. He eyed the story-teller with wonder and admiration, mouth wide open. 'Be careful, buddy, you'll be a-catching flies,' the sergeant said. The tattered man shrank back, ashamed.

After a time he began to draw nearer again to Henry, and to try to make friends with him. His voice was gentle, and there was a pleading look in his eyes. Henry saw with surprise that the man had two wounds, one in the head, bound with a blood-soaked rag, and the other in the arm, causing it to hang uselessly like a broken branch of a tree.

After they had walked together for some distance, the tattered man said, ' 'Twas a pretty good fight, wasn't it?' Henry glanced up at the blood-stained, grim face: 'Yes,' he said, and quickened his pace.

But the other hobbled persistently after him. There was an air of apology in his manner, but he evidently

45

thought that he needed only to talk for a time, and Henry would see what a good fellow he was.

'A pretty good fight, wasn't it?' he began again in a quiet voice, and then he continued: 'Darn me if I ever saw fellows fight so. I knew the boys would warm to it once they got square at it. The boys ain't had no fair chance up to now, but this time they showed what they was made of. I knew it would turn out right. You can't lick them boys. No, sir! They're fighters, they be.'

He paused for breath. He had looked at Henry for encouragement several times. He received none, but he seemed to get absorbed in his subject, and went on with his praise of 'the boys'.

'I was talking 'cross pickets, once, with a rebel boy from Georgia, and he says, "Your fellows'll all run like hell when once they hear the guns," he said. "Maybe they will," I said, "but I don't believe none of it," I said. "And, by jiminey," I says back to 'im, "Maybe your fellows'll all run like hell when once they hear the guns." I said. He laughed. 'Well, they didn't run today, did they, eh? No, sir! They fought, and fought, and fought.'

His homely face lit up with a light of love for the army, which was to him all things beautiful and powerful.

After a time, he turned to Henry again. 'Where was you hit, ol' boy?' he asked in a brotherly tone.

Henry felt instant panic at this question, although at first he did not realise the full import of it. 'What?' he asked.

'Where was you hit?' repeated the tattered man.

'Why,' began Henry, 'I—I—that is, —why—I—'

He turned away suddenly, and slipped through the crowd. His face was flushed, and his fingers picked

46

nervously at one of his buttons. He bent his head and fixed his eyes upon the button as if it were a little problem in itself.

The tattered man looked after him in astonishment.

Chapter 9

Henry fell back until the tattered soldier was not in sight, then he started to walk on with the others.

But he was amid wounds. The men were bleeding. Because of the tattered soldier's question he felt his shame must be obvious. He glanced sideways to see if anyone was staring at him. He rather envied the wounded men. He thought they must be happy. He wished that he too had a wound like them—a red badge of courage.

The soldier with the death-like pallor on his face walked with his eyes fixed in a stare into the unknown. Other men were trying to help him, give him advice, but he signed for them to go on and leave him alone. As he walked he seemed to be looking for somewhere to lie down. It was as if he was looking for a grave.

Something in the way the man waved the soldiers away from him made Henry suddenly start in horror. He tottered forward and laid a hand on the man's arm.

As the grey face turned towards him, he screamed: 'Gawd. Jim Conklin! It's you!'

The tall soldier gave a sort of smile. 'Hello, Henry,' he said.

The youth swayed on his feet and stared at his friend. He stammered over and over again. 'Oh, Jim—oh, Jim—oh, Jim—'

Jim held out his hand,covered with red and black, in a mixture of old and new blood upon it. 'Where've you been, Henry?' I thought maybe you'd been hit. There's been thunder to pay, today. I was worryin' about it.'

Henry could only lament. 'Oh, Jim—oh, Jim—oh, Jim—'

The tall soldier went on, 'Y' know, I was out there. And Lord, what a circus! And I got shot, by jiminey, I got shot. Yes, I sure got shot.'

Henry tried to help him, yet Jim went firmly along on some inner urge. But suddenly he seemed overcome by terror. His grey face was like paste. He began to speak in a whisper: 'I tell you what I'm afraid of, Henry. I'm afraid to fall down—and then those damned artillery wagons will run over me, like as not, and that's what I'm afraid of, Henry.'

The youth cried out hysterically, 'Oh, Jim, I'll take care of you. I swear to Gawd I will. I'll take care of you, Jim.'

'Will you, Henry—will you, sure?' Jim begged him.

'Yes, yes, I tell you. I'll take care of you, Jim, sure . . . ' Henry could hardly speak because of the gulps in his throat.

But Jim hung on to Henry's arm, and his eyes were wide in terror.

'I was always a good friend to you, Henry, wasn't I? And it ain't much to ask, is it? Just to pull me along

48

off the road; I'd do it for you, wouldn't I?'

Sobs came from Henry in anguish. He tried to express his feelings as he clung to Jim—somehow to show his concern and loyalty.

But Jim became again a grim grey figure with but one urge: to plod forward. Henry tried to make his friend lean on him, but Jim only protested: 'No, no, Henry, leave me be, leave me be.' His look was fixed again upon the unknown. He moved with a mysterious purpose. 'No, leave me be, leave me be!'

Henry had to follow. Presently the voice of the tattered soldier came softly from near his shoulder, 'You'd better take 'im off the road, pardner. There's a battery coming soon and he'll get runned over, maybe. He's a goner anyway, you can see that. Take him out of the road . . . '

Henry grasped Jim by the arm. 'Jim, Jim, come with me.'

Jim stared at him for a moment. Then he seemed to understand, 'Oh—into the fields—oh—'

The galloping horses and lashing riders of the battery clattered past.

Suddenly Jim began to run in a staggering, stumbling way towards some bushes. Henry ran after him, pleading with him: 'Jim, what are you doing! You'll hurt yourself. Stay with me.'

Jim had his eyes fixed on some unknown purpose. 'Leave me be, can't you? Leave me be for a minnit . . . ' He staggered away by himself.

Henry and the tattered soldier followed, helpless and yet concerned. It seemed as if the wounded man was intent on some last rite of his own. At last they saw him stop and stand motionless. His face seemed calm, as if he had found what he wanted, something that he had come to meet. They stood in silence as he waited.

Then Jim's chest began to heave and strain. It was as if an animal was within him, kicking and struggling to be free.

Henry sank wailing to the ground, calling 'Jim—oh, Jim—oh, Jim.'

Jim spoke again. His spare figure was now upright, his bloody hands were quietly by his side. He was waiting, as if for a summons. He said, 'Leave me be, don't touch me, leave me be!'

There was another silence while he waited.

Suddenly his whole body shook. He seemed to be caught in a terrible strangeness that enveloped him. His tall figure stretched itself to his full height. Then it began to swing forward, slow and straight, in the manner of a falling tree. As it fell, the left shoulder struck the ground first, and the body seemed to bounce a little way from the earth before it lay still.

Henry had been watching his friend, spellbound, at this ceremony of Jim's meeting with death. He now sprang to his feet and went closer to gaze upon Jim's face. The mouth was open and the teeth showed in a deathly grin. It was the end.

As the flap of Jim's blue jacket fell away from the body, Henry could see that one side looked as if it had been chewed by wolves.

Henry turned with sudden mad rage towards the battle-field. He shook his fist. He seemed about to deliver an endless curse.

'Hell,' he screamed.

The fierce red eye of the setting sun seemed to reflect his helpless anger.

Chapter 10

The tattered man stood, thinking.

'Well, he was a regular jim-dandy for nerve, wasn't he?' he said finally in a quiet, awestruck voice. 'A regular jim-dandy. I wonder where he got his strength from. I never seen a man do like that before. It was a funny thing. Well, he was a regular jim-dandy.'

Henry wanted to cry out in grief, but he was struck dumb. He threw himself upon the ground and brooded.

The tattered man stood looking at him, and, after a time said, 'Look here, pardner,'—and while he thus addressed Henry, he had one eye on the corpse. 'He's a goner, ain't he, and we might as well begin to look after ourselves. This 'ere thing's all over. He's gone, ain't he? And he's all right here. No body'll bother him. And I must say I ain't enjoying any great health myself just now.'

Henry, roused by the tattered soldier's tone, looked up quickly. He saw that his companion was swaying uncertainly on his legs and that his face had turned blue.

'Good Lord,' he cried, 'you ain't going to—not you, too?'

The tattered man waved his hand. 'Not to die,' he said. 'All I want is some pea soup and a good bed. Some pea soup,' he repeated, as if in a dream.

Henry rose from the ground. 'I wonder where he came from,' he said. 'I left him over there.' He pointed. 'And now I found him here. And he was coming from over there, too,' He pointed in a new direction. They both turned towards the body, as if to ask it a question.

'Well,' said the tattered man at length, 'there ain't no use in our staying here and trying to ask him anything.'

Henry murmured something, to which the tattered man said, as if in reply: 'Well, he was a jim-dandy, wasn't he?'

They turned their back upon the corpse and stole softly away, on tiptoe.

For a time neither spoke, and then the tattered man broke the silence. 'I'm beginning to feel pretty bad. I'm beginning to feel pretty bad.'

Henry groaned, 'Oh Lord!' He wondered if he was going to have to witness another grim encounter with death. But his companion waved his hand reassuringly. 'Oh, I ain't going to die yet! There's too much depending on me for me to die yet. No, sir! Can't die! I *can't*! You ought to see the squad of children I've got, and all like that.'

Henry glanced at his companion, and could see by the shadow of a smile on his face that he was trying to make some fun out of the situation.

As they plodded on, the tattered soldier continued to talk. 'Besides, if I died, I wouldn't die the way that fellow did. That was the strangest thing. I'd just flop down, I would. I never see a fellow die the way that fellow did.'

'You know Tom Jamison, he lives next door to me at home. He's a nice fellow—smart, too. Well, when we were fighting this afternoon, all of a sudden he began to yell at me: "You're shot," he cried. I put up my hand to my head, and when I looked at my fingers, I saw, sure enough, I was shot. I gave a cry and began to run, but before I could get away another one hit me in the arm, and whirled me clean around. I got scared then, and I ran like hell, but I caught it pretty bad. I've an idea that I'd be fighting yet, if it wasn't for Tom Jamison.'

Then he said calmly: 'There's two of them—little ones, but they're beginning to have fun with me now. I don't believe I can walk much farther.'

They went slowly on in silence. 'You look pretty peeked yourself,' said the tattered man, at last. 'I bet you got a worse one than you think. You'd better take care of your hurt. It don't do to let such things go. It might be inside mostly, and then it's real bad. Where is your wound?'

The tattered man continued to **prattle** on without waiting for a reply. 'I see a fellow get hit right in the head, when my regiment was standing at ease once. Everybody yelled out at him. Hurt, John? Are you hurt much? "No," says he. He looked kind of surprised. Said he didn't feel nothing. But, Gawd, the next thing that fellow knew he was dead. So you want to watch out! You might have some queer kind of hurt yourself. You never can tell. Where *are* you hurt?'

Henry had been uncomfortable ever since his companion had brought the matter up. Now he was angry and cried, 'Oh, don't bother me!' He was furious with the tattered man and could have strangled him. His companions always seemed to succeed in making him feel a sense of shame. 'Now, don't bother me,' he repeated, threateningly.

'Well, Lord knows, I don't want to bother anybody,' said the other. 'Lord knows, I've got enough troubles of my own,' he added despairingly.

Henry, who had been wondering how he could rid himself of this man whom he had come now almost to hate, spoke in a hard voice as he hurried away: 'Good-bye.'

The tattered man looked after him amazed. 'Why—why, pardner, where are you going?' he asked unsteadily. Henry, looking back at him, could see that he, too, like that other one, was beginning to act dumb and animal-like. His mind seemed to be wandering. 'Now—now—look here—you, Tom Jamison—now I won't have this—this won't do. Where—where—you going?'

Henry pointed vaguely. 'Over there,' he replied.

'Well, now look—a—here, now,' said the tattered man, rambling on in idiot fashion. His head was hanging forward, and his words were slurred. 'This thing won't do, now, Tom Jamison. It won't do. I know you, you pig-headed devil. You want to go tramping off with a bad hurt. It ain't right, Tom Jamison. You want to let me take care of you, Tom Jamison. It ain't right—you—with a bad hurt—it ain't right—it ain't—'

Henry took no notice and climbed a fence to get away. He could hear the tattered man crying **plaintively**, and once he turned about angrily, calling, 'What?'

'Look—a—here, now, Tom Jamison—now—it ain't—'

Henry went on. Turning once again, when some distance away, he saw the tattered man wandering about helplessly in the field.

He now thought he wished he was dead. The simple questions of the tattered man had been like knife thrusts at him. They made him feel that he could not keep his crime hidden much longer. It was sure to be discovered, and he admitted to himself that he had no defence.

Chapter 11

He became aware that the roar of battle was getting louder. Great brown clouds floated in the air before him. The noise, too, was coming nearer, and more men seemed to be in the fields.

As he rounded a small hill, he saw that the roadway was now a **seething** mass of wagons, horses and men. There were loud shouts, commands and curses. Fear was sweeping them all along. Horses plunged and tugged under the cracking whips.

Henry felt in some measure cheered by the sight. They must all be retreating. Perhaps he wasn't so bad after all!

Presently a column of infantry appeared in the road like a serpent making its way between the mass of wagons and horses. Men at the head of the column were prodding mules with their muskets. They were forcing a way through the throng by brute strength. The backs of the officers were rigid. They were leading their men to confront the enemy with pride and determination; the importance of the thrust forward was written on their grave and stern faces.

As Henry saw this determined movement, his black woe returned to him. He was watching a procession of chosen beings who marched as if with weapons of flame. He could never be like them, and yet he longed to be worthy of them. The haste of the march forward seemed in some way to be finer than the mere fighting. Such heroes could feel that they had done their best— kept their self-respect, whatever happened.

He wondered what these men had eaten to enable them to force their way towards battle and death with such power. His envy of them made him wish to change places with them. He saw himself leading the column—a desperate figure with sword carried high, getting calmly killed in front of them all, his dead body a glorious sacrifice. For a moment he was up-lifted by the glory of war, the thought of victory.

Then suddenly, his doubts and difficulties returned, and he hesitated on one foot. He had no rifle, he could not fight with his hands, and where was his regiment?

But rifles were available all around him, and he could fight with any regiment. His face would be hidden in the ranks of battle.

Yet his companions would see through his lies, he could not maintain a heroic stand. He suddenly fell headlong, feeling that his strength had gone.

In his emotion and struggle he had not been much aware of his aches and pains, but he now discovered that he had a scorching thirst. His face was dry and dirty and his skin seemed to crackle. Every bone in his body ached, and his feet were like two sores. Also his body was calling for food. It was more than mere hunger. It felt like a great weight in his stomach. When he tried to walk again, his head swayed and he stumbled. He could not see properly and his eyes seemed covered by a green mist.

In his despair he knew in his heart that he would never be a hero; he was too much of a coward. His pictures of glory were not real. He groaned and stag-gered, still trying to keep near the scene of the struggle. He still wanted to know who was winning.

He told his conscience that many men of courage turned and ran from the enemy, and he would not have run any faster than they. Previously there had been many defeats in the recent months, and always the people had blamed the army at first, but they soon

changed their opinions to praise the valour of uncon-
quered men.

Besides, in a defeat he saw himself **vindicated**. It
would prove that he had fled early in the battle
because of his superior powers of foresight. A serious
prophet expecting a flood would be the first to climb a
tree. It would prove that he was indeed a prophet.

As these thoughts went through his mind, Henry
knew that he was really selfish and wrong. He was a
villain at heart. He wished he was dead. He envied
those who had died. Yet he had been taught that the
mighty **blue machine of war** would be victorious. It
was the eternal creed of soldiers. Utter defeat was
impossible.

Yet he was still afraid of the arrow of scorn that
might be aimed at him when he rejoined his comrades.
He imagined the whole regiment saying: 'Where's
Henry Fleming? He did run, didn't he? He did run,
for sure?'

There would be no peace for him under the questions
and the sneers. In the next fight they would watch him
more closely. Wherever he went in camp he would
meet the cruel stares, the sneering remarks: 'There he
goes—'

He would never live it down. Their faces would
always turn towards him with wide, cruel grins. They
would always jeer at him. They would never forget.

Chapter 12

The column that had pushed its way forward through the disorderly mob along the roadway was hardly out of sight, when Henry saw further waves of men come sweeping out of the woods. They came down upon him, a ragged and untidy mob. They looked as if their spirits had been crushed. He knew at once that here were more men whose courage had failed them, and who were now retreating from the battle. He supposed the fight must be lost. The army, helpless in the thickets of the wood and blinded by the oncoming night, was going to be destroyed. Could it really be so?

Something within him made him cry out. He felt he ought to try to rally the men, or even sing a battle hymn, but all he could manage was: 'Why—why— what— what's happened?'

Soon he was surrounded by the fleeing men. Henry turned from one to another as they sped past him, but they paid no attention to his appeals; they did not even seem to notice him.

Some of them were talking insanely. One huge man seemed to be demanding of the sky: 'Say, where's the darn road? Where's the darn road?' It was as if he had lost a child. He wept in his dismay.

Presently, men were running here and there in all directions. The guns booming away to the left and right, and forward and in the rear, added to the confusion, and the gathering darkness made it even more difficult to keep a sense of direction. Henry began to feel he had somehow got into the centre of the tremendous conflict, and he could see no way out of it.

After rushing about and shouting questions at the

retreating soldiers, Henry finally clutched a man by the arm. They swung round face to face. 'Why—why' stammered Henry, trying to find words to express his anxiety.

The man yelled at him: 'Let go me! Let go me!' as he tried to free himself from Henry's hold. His face was red and his eyes rolled wildly. He was panting and heaving. He still had his rifle and he tugged frantically to get away, so that Henry was dragged several paces. 'Let go me—let go me!' he cried again.'

'Why—why—' stammered Henry.

'Well, then,' shouted the man in a rage; and with that he fiercely swung his rifle. It crashed upon the youth's head. The man ran on.

There was a lightning flash before Henry's eyes, and a deafening roar in his head. Suddenly his legs gave way and he sank to the ground. He tried to get up, but in his efforts he was like a boxer felled by a knock-out blow. Sometimes he would manage to stand half upright, snatch at the air, and then fall back again clutching at the grass. His face was of a deathly pallor, and he groaned in his agony.

At last, with a twisting movement, he got on his hands and knees, and from thence, like a baby, struggled to his feet. Pressing his hands to his head, he lurched over the grass. He imagined some quiet place where, like Jim in his final struggle, he could fall and be undisturbed.

Once he put his hand to the top of his head and timidly touched the wound. The pain made him draw a long breath through clenched teeth. His fingers were spotted with blood, and he looked at them with a fixed stare.

Around him he could hear the rumble of gun-carriages, as horses dragged them towards the front. Once, a young officer on a mud-spattered horse nearly ran him down. He turned and watched the mass of guns, men and horses sweeping in a wide curve towards a gap in a fence. The artillery were assembling, as if for a conference.

The blue haze of evening was upon the field. The lines of the forest were long purple shadows. One cloud lay along the western sky, partly smothering the red glow of the sunset.

As Henry left the scene behind him, he heard the guns suddenly roar again. The air was filled with their tremendous noise, and with it came the din of rifle fire. Turning to look behind him, he could see sheets of orange flame light up the darkening sky.

He hurried on in the dusk. The daylight had now faded so much that he could hardly see where he was going. But the forest was filled with men, and he could hear their voices and vaguely make out their forms in the darkness.

His wound now pained him only a little, but he was afraid to move quickly for fear of disturbing it. His thoughts, as he walked, were fixed intently upon his hurt. There was a cool liquid feeling about it, and he imagined blood oozing slowly down under his hair. His head seemed swollen to a size too big for his neck to bear.

And then he began to remember various things which had happened in the past. He thought of certain meals his mother had cooked at home of those dishes of which he was particularly fond. He saw the spread table, and the pine walls of the kitchen glowing in the warm light from the stove. He remembered, too, how he and his companions used to go from the schoolhouse to a shaded pool to bathe. He felt the cool fragrance of the water on his body.

He was overcome presently by utter weariness. His head hung forward and his shoulders drooped. His feet shuffled along the ground. He kept asking himself whether he should lie down and sleep, or force himself on till he reached a safer place. At last he heard a cheery voice near his shoulder: 'You seem to be in a pretty bad way, boy.' Henry did not look up, but he murmured assent with a groan.

The owner of the cheery voice took him firmly by the arm. 'Well,' he said with a laugh, 'I'm going your way. The whole gang of us is going your way. I guess I can help you along.'

They began to walk together like a drunken man and his friend.

As they went along, the man questioned Henry, and anticipated his replies like one guiding the mind of a child.

'What regiment do you belong to, eh? What's that? Oh, the 304th New York? Why, what corps is that in? Oh, it is? Why, I thought they weren't engaged today. They're way over in the centre. Oh, they were, were they?

'Well, pretty nearly everybody got their share of fighting today. Gawd, I gave myself up for dead any number of times. There was shooting here and shooting there, and hollering here and hollering there, in the damn darkness, until I couldn't tell which damn side I was on. It was the most mixed up darn thing I ever saw.

'And these 'ere woods are in a right old mess. It'll be a miracle if we find our regiments tonight. How did you get way over here, anyhow? Your regiment is a long way from here, ain't it? Well, I guess we can find it. It'll be long hunting, but I guess we can do it.'

In the search that followed, the man with the cheery voice seemed to Henry to possess a magic wand. He found his way through the tangled forest with uncanny skill. When they ran into guards and patrols he displayed the keenness of mind of a detective, and the pluck of a street urchin. If there were obstacles, he turned them to advantage. Henry, with his chin on his chest, watched while his companion made light of the most **obstinate** difficulties.

The forest seemed to be a hive of men buzzing about in aimless circles, but the cheery man guided Henry without missing his way, until at last he began to chuckle with glee and self-satisfaction. 'Ah, there you are! See the fire?' Henry nodded. 'Well, there's where your regiment is. And now, good-bye, old boy; and good luck to you.'

Henry felt a warm and strong hand clasp his limp fingers for an instant, and then he heard a cheerful whistle as the man strode away. As this good friend left him, it suddenly occurred to Henry that he had not once seen his face.

Chapter 13

Henry went slowly towards the fire in the distance. As he staggered on, he wondered what sort of welcome his comrades would give him—maybe it might be one of ridicule. Well, he had no strength left to invent a tale. He would be an easy target.

He thought perhaps he could still get away and hide, but he felt too weak and exhausted. He must have food and rest, whatever the cost. He went unsteadily on. He could see the shadows of men moving in the firelight. As he got nearer he could see dim rows of sleeping soldiers.

Suddenly he was confronted by a sentry. 'Halt!' came from a black shape. A rifle barrel shone in the light from the fire. He thought he recognised the voice. He called out, 'Why, hello, Wilson, is that you here?'

The rifle was lowered and Wilson came slowly forward, peering: 'Is that you, Henry?'

'Yes, yes, it's me.'

'Well, well, ol' boy,' said the other. 'Am I glad to see you! By ginger, I gave you up for a goner! I thought you was dead, sure enough.'

Henry could hardly stand; he felt weak and defenceless. He felt he must explain his presence at once, to avoid awkward questions.

'Yes, yes, it's me. I've had an awful time. I've been all over the place—over on the right, terrible fighting—I had an awful time. I got separated from everybody. I got shot, in the head. I never see such fighting. I got shot.'

Wilson came forward. 'What—you got shot? Why didn't you say so before? Poor old boy. We must see. Hold on a minnit, I'll call Simpson.'

Another figure came near. It was the corporal, Simpson. 'Who are you talking to, Wilson? Why, hello Henry. You here? I thought you was dead hours ago. Why, they keep turning up. We thought we'd lost forty-two, but if they keep on comin' we'll have a company by the morning yet! Where were you?'

'Over on the right,' said Henry at once. 'I got separated . . . '

Wilson went on, 'Yes, and he got shot in the head, and we must see to him right away.' He put his arm round Henry's shoulder. 'Gee, it must hurt like thunder!'

Henry leaned against him. 'Yes, it hurts. Hurts a good bit,' he **faltered**.

The corporal held Henry's arm. 'Come on, boy, I'll take care of you.'

Wilson called after them, 'Put him to sleep on my blanket, Simpson, and—hold on a minnit—here's my bottle. It's got coffee in it. Have a look at his head and see how it is. When I get relieved in a while, I'll come and see to him.'

Henry's knees shook. The corporal led him into the firelight. 'Now let's have a look at your old head.'

The youth sat down obediently, and the corporal began to look for the wound in Henry's bushy hair.

'Ah, here we are,' he said, whistling through his teeth as he found the blood and the signs of injury. 'Just as I thought, you've been grazed by a bullet. It's raised a lump just as if someone hit you on the head with a club, but it's stopped bleeding. In the morning you'll feel that a number ten hat wouldn't fit you, but you never can tell. Now you just sit here, and I'll send Wilson to look after you.'

Henry remained where he was, staring at the fire. He saw men sprawled all round, sleeping in **oblivion**.

On the other side of the fire, there was a tall officer asleep, seated upright with his back against a tree. He was the picture of an exhausted soldier.

Soon Wilson came along, swinging two bottles by their straps. 'Well, now, Henry, ol' boy,' he said. 'We'll have you fixed up in no time.'

He bustled about like an amateur nurse. He made his patient drink deeply of the coffee. Henry tilted his head back and let the coffee slip down his throat. Then he sighed in deep relief.

Wilson produced a large handkerchief which he folded like a bandage, and wetted it with water from the other bottle. He bound this round Henry's head and tied the end of it at the back of his neck.

'There,' said Wilson. 'You look pretty awful, but I bet you feel better!'

Henry looked at his friend with grateful eyes. The cool cloth was like a woman's tender hand upon his aching head.

'You didn't holler much,' said Wilson. 'I'm not much good at taking care of sick folks, and you never squeaked. Most men with a wound like that would have been in hospital by now. A shot in the head is no fool business!'

Henry made no reply, but began to undo the buttons of his jacket.

'Come on,' continued Wilson. 'I must put you to bed and see you get a good night's rest.'

He led Henry among the sleeping forms, and picked up his blankets. He spread the rubber one upon the ground, and placed the woollen one around the youth's shoulders.

Henry began to lie down, the ground feeling to him like a soft bed. But he suddenly cried, 'Hold on a minnit. Where you going to sleep? I've got your . . . '

His friend waved his hand. 'Right there by you, don't worry; shut up and go to sleep.'

Henry said no more. A delightful drowsiness had come over him. The warm comfort of the blanket enveloped him. His head fell forward on his arm, and his eyes closed. He gave a long sigh, snuggled down into the blanket, and in a moment was fast asleep.

Chapter 14

When Henry awoke, it seemed to him that he had been asleep for a thousand years. As he opened his eyes, everything around him seemed strange. A cold dew chilled his face, causing him to snuggle further down under his blanket. He stared for a while at the leaves of the trees overhead, now being stirred by the early morning breeze.

Already there was the noise of fighting in the distance, a deadly persistent sound, as if it had been going on for ever and was not to cease.

All around him were rows and groups of men whom he dimly remembered seeing the previous night. They were snatching their last bit of sleep before the call to duty.

He heard the noise of a fire crackling, and turning his head, saw Wilson busily tending it. A few other figures moved in the mist, and he heard the sound of axe blows, as men chopped wood.

Suddenly there was a rumble of drums, and a distant bugle could be heard. Similar sounds, some loud, some faint, came from far and near all over the forest. Those that still slept were being roused for the new day's work. As they stirred from their sleep, there was much grumbling and swearing at the early hours that war demanded of them. A sharp command from an officer rang out, and soon every man was on his feet, ready to face what the day might bring.

Henry sat up and yawned. He rubbed his eyes, and then, putting his hand to his head, felt carefully the bandage over his wound. Wilson, seeing he was awake, came over to him from the fire. 'Well, Henry, ol' man, how do you feel this morning?' he enquired.

Henry yawned again. In truth, his wound felt very sore, and he had an uneasy feeling in his stomach. 'Oh, Lord, I feel pretty bad,' he said.

'Thunder!' exclaimed Wilson. 'I hoped you'd feel much better this morning. Let's see the bandage. I guess it's slipped.' He began to feel around the wound rather clumsily, until Henry protested, 'Dammit! You're the clumsiest man I ever saw. Why can't you be more careful?' He glared at Wilson, who answered quietly, 'Well, well, come now and get some grub. Then, maybe, you'll feel better.'

At the fireside Wilson watched over his friend with care. He busily arranged the tin mugs and poured into them a steaming rust-coloured brew from a small, smoky tin can. He had some fresh meat, which he roasted on a stick. Then he sat down and happily watched Henry enjoy the meal he had got ready for him.

Henry noticed what a remarkable change had come over Wilson since those earlier days of camp life on the river bank. He seemed no longer to be forever boasting. He did not now so easily take offence at what might be said to him. He had become quietly confident in himself. He was, in fact, no longer the 'loud soldier'.

Wilson balanced his mug of coffee on his knee. 'Well, Henry,' he said, 'what do you think our chances are? Do you think we'll wallop 'em?'

Henry thought for a moment. Finally, he replied, 'Day before yesterday, you'd have bet you'd lick the whole lot of 'em by yourself.'

His friend looked rather surprised. 'Would I?' he asked. Then he thought a while and said, as he gazed into the fire, 'Well, perhaps I would.'

Henry was, in his turn, surprised by Wilson's reply, and tried to make **amends** by saying, 'Oh, no, you wouldn't, really.'

But Wilson smiled and said, 'Oh, you needn't mind, Henry; I believe I was rather a fool in those days.' He spoke as if it was years ago.

There was a pause and then Wilson continued: 'All the officers say we've got the rebels in a pretty tight corner. They all seem to think we've got 'em just where we want 'em.'

'I don't know about that,' Henry replied. 'What I saw over on the right makes me think it was the other way about. From where I was, it looked as if we were getting a good pounding yesterday.'

'Do you think so?' said Wilson. 'I thought we gave 'em a pretty rough time yesterday.'

'Not a bit,' replied Henry. 'Why, Lord, man, you didn't see nothing of the fight. Why!' Then a sudden thought came to him. 'Oh, Jim Conklin's dead.'

His friend was shocked. 'What? Is he? Jim Conklin?'

Henry spoke slowly: 'Yes. He's dead. Shot in the side.'

'You don't say so. Jim Conklin; poor devil,' said Wilson.

All about them were other small fires surrounded by groups of men having their breakfast. From one of these groups came voices raised in a quarrel. It appeared that two young soldiers had been teasing a huge bearded man, causing him to spill coffee over his knees. The man had jumped up in rage and was swearing loudly at the young men. Stung by the bearded man's language, the two had taken great offence. It looked as if there was going to be a fight.

Wilson got up and went over to them, and tried to make peace. 'Oh, here, now, boys, what's the use?' he said. 'We'll be at the rebels in less than an hour. What's the good of fighting amongst ourselves?'

One of the young soldiers turned upon him, red-faced and angry. 'You needn't come around here with your preaching. I suppose you don't approve of fighting since Charlie Morgan licked you! And I don't see what business this is of yours, anyway.'

'Well, it ain't,' said Wilson, mildly. 'Still I hate to see you boys fall out.'

Wilson returned to his seat. Henry laughed at him, saying, 'You've changed a good bit. You ain't at all like you used to be.'

'No, I suppose I have changed,' said his friend, thoughtfully.

'Well, I didn't mean . . . ' began Henry.

'Oh, you needn't mind, Henry,' said Wilson, and then, after a pause, he went on: 'The regiment lost over half the men yesterday. I thought, of course, they were all dead, but, Lord, they kept coming back last night, until, it seems, after all, we lost only a few. They'd been scattered all over, wandering around in the woods, fighting alongside other regiments—just like you done.'

'Is that so?' said Henry.

Chapter 15

Later, when the regiment was standing at the side of a lane, waiting for the order to march, Henry remembered the little packet that Wilson had entrusted to him some days ago. He uttered an exclamation and turned to his companion: 'Wilson!'

'What?' His friend was staring down the lane, his thoughts elsewhere.

'Oh, nothing,' Henry said. Wilson turned to him. 'What was you going to say?' he asked.

'Oh, nothing,' repeated Henry. He didn't want to upset his friend by mention of the packet now.

It was a small weapon he decided to keep in reserve. Wilson had spoken of his possible death with much emotion in a weak moment, but Henry now decided to keep it unmentioned for some time. The packet was a secret advantage, and he felt proud that he had been entrusted with it.

He had shown weakness himself in some ways of late, perhaps, but not to the extent of Wilson's sorrow and fear at the thought of his possible death, when he had handed over the package. He had really delivered himself into Henry's hands because of his weakness.

Henry felt scorn for all those who were weak in this way, and he now felt superior to Wilson. His own self-pride was restored, and no one need know of his 'desertion' in battle, and his disappearance from the ranks. It was not likely that the truth would be discovered now, and he felt strong and proud like a veteran.

Henry didn't much worry now about the battles ahead of them, or how he would behave in future. He remembered how some of the men had run with such terror-stricken faces. Surely they had been more wild and frightened than was necessary? He himself had kept his head, and had managed better and with more dignity.

He was aroused from this **reverie** by Wilson, who had been in a **fidget** under the trees. He suddenly coughed and came near to speak to him: 'Fleming!'

'What?'

Wilson put his hand to his mouth and coughed again.

'Well,' he gulped, 'I guess you might as well give me back them letters now.' His face and brow were flushed, and he was pulling at his collar as he spoke.

'All right, Wilson,' Henry said. He loosened two buttons of his jacket, thrust in his hand, and brought out the packet. As he passed it over, his friend's face was turned away from him.

71

Henry had been slow to hand over the packet, because he could think of nothing to say. So he allowed Wilson to escape with his packet without too much awkwardness.

Wilson seemed to be suffering a sort of shame, and Henry felt himself the stronger by comparison. He had never felt the need to blush for anything he did. He was different.

He reflected with a sort of pity, 'Too bad! The poor devil. It's made him feel darned awkward.'

Later, as they marched, Henry began to think about how he'd feel on returning home. He felt quite competent to arouse the interest of all who heard his stories of the war. He could see himself the centre of attraction as he reported various incidents.

He imagined the concern and amazement of his mother and the dark young lady of the seminary as they drank it all in. There was nothing like stories of brave deeds on the field of battle to please the ladies.

Chapter 16

All this time the sound of rifle and gun fire could be heard. Henry's regiment was marched to relieve troops that had been in trenches for a long time, defending a position. They took their places behind a curving line of rifle pits, and took turns at manning the earthwork defences.

Whilst awaiting their turn, Henry and Wilson faced away from the firing and tried to relax. Wilson lay down, buried his face in his arms, and went to sleep. Henry, however, remained standing, and leaning against the dirt wall of the trench, peered over at the woods, and up and down the line.

Although the guns to the right and left continued to make an awful din, Henry found the comparative quiet of the trenches strange. He wanted to make a joke about it, something like, 'All quiet on the **Rappananock**'—rather like a headline he had once seen in a newspaper. But the noise of the guns was so loud, he wouldn't have been heard if he had spoken.

At last the guns stopped, and rumours spread amongst the men in the rifle pits. Stories of doubts and hesitation on the part of those in command, even of a disastrous defeat, were passed along the line. Increased rifle fire from the enemy lines on the right seemed to confirm their fears. The men were disheartened and began to mutter. 'Oh, what more can we do?'

But before midday the regiment was being marched away again, retiring in good order through the woods. Enemy soldiers could be seen advancing across the fields, running and yelling. The sight of them enraged Henry and made him exclaim: 'by jiminey, we've got a lot of **block-heads** in command of us.'

'You're not the first to have said that today,' said a man near him. Wilson, who had had to be roused from his sleep, was still drowsy. When he realised what was happening, he remarked gloomily, 'Oh, well, I suppose we got licked.'

Henry was annoyed by Wilson's words, but didn't say so. Instead, he began to condemn the general. Wilson interrupted him: 'Maybe, it wasn't all his fault. He did the best he could. It's our bad luck to get licked so often.'

'Well, don't we fight like the devil? Don't we do all that we possibly can?' demanded Henry.

No one questioned Henry's right to speak like this, and he went on to repeat something he had heard at the camp that morning: 'The brigadier said he never saw a regiment fight the way we fought yesterday. And we didn't do any better than many another regiment, did we? Well, then, you can't say it's the army's fault, can you?'

Wilson answered, 'Of course, not. No man dare say we don't fight like the devil. But still, we don't have no luck.'

'Well, then, if we fight like the devil, and don't ever win, it must be the general's fault,' said Henry firmly.

A man marching at Henry's side said sarcastically, 'Maybe you think you fought the whole battle yesterday, Fleming.'

These words alarmed Henry, who thought the man must know about him running away. 'Why, no,' he hastened to say, 'I don't think that.'

But apparently the other had no such suspicion, and merely replied, 'Oh!' Nevertheless, Henry felt a threat. The sarcastic man's words put a stop to his brave talk, and he remained silent after that.

The noise of firing dogged their footsteps. The men were uneasy, and the officers impatient and short-tempered. At last, in a clear space in the woods, the troops were halted, and lines were reformed to face the pursuing enemy infantry.

As the sun climbed high in the sky, the attack started and the woods crackled with the sound of rifle fire.

'I was willing to bet they'd attack as soon as the sun was fully up,' said the lieutenant, who was in charge of Henry's company. He strode to and fro in the rear of his men, who were lying down behind whatever protection they could find.

Henry began to grumble again. 'Good Gawd,' he complained, 'we're always being chased around like rats. It makes me sick. I'd like to know why in thunder we were marched into these woods, anyhow, unless it was to give the rebels another chance to take pot shots at us. It's this darned old fool of a general.'

Wilson interrupted his friend. 'It'll turn out all right in the end,' he said.

'Oh, the devil it will! You always talk like a darned old parson. Don't tell me! I know . . .'

The lieutenant cut him short. 'You boys shut up! There's no need to waste your breath arguing about this, that, and the other. All you've got to do is fight, and you'll get plenty of that to do in about ten minutes. Less talking and more fighting is what's wanted from you boys.' He continued to pace up and down, and as there was no more argument, he paused for a final remark: 'There's too much **chin-wagging** and too little fighting in this war, anyhow.'

Now the firing immediately in front of the regiment increased. The guns in the rear opened up, answering those behind the enemy lines. The battle roar became like rolling thunder, a single, long explosion.

The men of the 304th were worn out and exhausted, having slept little and laboured long the day before. They stood awaiting the shock of the attack.

Chapter 17

As the army advanced, Henry began to burn with rage. He wanted to sit down and think, but the enemy seemed determined to give him no rest. Yesterday he had fought and fled, and there had been many adventures. Surely today he'd earned some relief and rest. He was sore and stiff after yesterday's exertions, and he felt he was owed some time to himself.

But those other men seemed never to grow weary. They fought at their own speed; they were a relentless foe.

Henry leaned forward and spoke to Wilson. 'If they keep on chasin' us, by Gawd, they'd better watch —we can't stand too much of it.'

Wilson made a calm reply. 'If they keep on chasin' us, they'll drive us all into the river.'

Henry cried out savagely at this. He crouched behind a tree with his eyes burning and his teeth clenched. The bandage was still round his head, and dried blood showed over the wound. His jacket and shirt were open at the throat, and his tanned neck was exposed.

If only he could get near to the enemy and hit them with his fists! His fingers clung tightly to his rifle. He wished he could wipe out the foe with his deadly fire. He lost sense of anything but his hate—his desire to smash the smiles of victory on the faces of his enemies!

The heat of smoke and flame seemed to burn his skin. His rifle barrel got so hot that he could hardly bear it, but he kept stuffing cartridges into it and pounding them in with his iron ramrod. Every time he pulled the trigger he gave a fierce grunt, as if he was hitting the foe with all his strength.

When the enemy seemed to fall back, he went forward after them like a dog chasing its foe. Once he was firing almost alone when those near him had ceased—he had not been aware of the lull.

He was shouted at by a soldier next to him, 'You fool! Why don't you quit when there ain't nothin' to shoot at? Good Gawd!'

Henry suddenly realised that the ground ahead was empty of enemy figures; his fellows were staring at him in astonishment.

He threw himself on the ground like a man that had been thrashed. He groped for his water bottle.

The lieutenant was crowing; he seemed drunk with fighting. He called out to Henry: 'By heavens, if I had ten thousand wild cats like you, I could finish off this war in less than a week!'

Some of the men muttered and looked at Henry. He had gone on loading and firing, and cursing like a madman. They now looked upon him as a real war devil.

Wilson came staggering along. 'Are you all right,

Henry? How do you feel? There ain't nothing the matter with you, is there?'

'No, of course not,' said Henry. His throat seemed sore and dry. He must have seemed like an animal to the others. He now felt quite a hero. And yet he had not known what he was doing. He lay back and relaxed on the ground.

'Well, they lost a pile of men, they did,' said a voice.
'*A dog, a woman, and a walnut tree,*
The more you beat 'em, the better they be!'
said another. 'That's just like us!'

'Hot work! hot work!' cried the lieutenant, very pleased. He walked up and down, laughing and praising his men. 'By thunder, I bet this army'll never see another new regiment like this! By thunder, boys, you've done fine!'

Chapter 18

During the lull in the fighting, the regiment had some rest for a few minutes. One man had been shot through the body, and, as the firing died down, his cries of pain could be heard. Perhaps, he had been calling out for some time, but no one could have heard him above the din. Now the men turned to see who it was.

'Who is it? Who is it?'

'It's Jimmy Rogers. Jimmy Rogers.'

The wounded man was twisting about in the grass and screaming, as if in a fit. No one seemed to know what to do, and the poor man was cursing them for not helping him.

Wilson had an idea that there was a stream near by, and he got permission to go for some water. Immediately, water bottles were thrust at him: 'Fill mine, will you? Bring me some, too. And me, too.' He went away, loaded down with bottles. Henry went with him, thinking how good it would be to dip his hands and face in the stream, and to have a long drink of water at the same time.

They made a hurried search for the stream, but did not find it. 'No water here,' said Henry, so they had to turn back disappointed. From their position, as they again faced towards the fighting, they were able to see a lot more of the battle ground.

Looking down a clearing between some trees, Henry and Wilson saw a general and his staff officer almost ride over a wounded man, who was crawling about on his hands and knees. The general checked his horse just in time, but a moment later the wounded man's strength failed him, and he fell, sliding over on his back.

Very soon, the general and his attendant were almost directly in front of Henry and Wilson. Another officer, riding with the skill of a cowboy, galloped his horse up to the general. The two young soldiers had not been noticed, and lingered close by in the hope of overhearing what might be said. Perhaps, they thought, some important plan of action was to be discussed.

The general, whom the boys recognised as the commander of their division, looked at the officer and said: 'The enemy's forming over there for another charge. It will be directed against Whiterside, and I fear they'll break through, unless we do our damnedest to stop them.'

The officer answered briefly, 'There'll be hell to pay, stopping them!'

'I expect so,' replied the general. Then he began to talk in a lower tone of voice, illustrating his words by pointing his finger. Henry and Wilson could not hear anything until the general asked: 'What troops can you spare?'

The officer thought for a moment. 'Well,' he said, 'I had to order in the 12th to help the 76th, and I haven't really got any. But there's the 304th. They fight like a lot of mule drivers. I can spare them best of any.'

Henry and Wilson looked at each other in astonishment. The general gave a sharp order: 'Get them ready, then. I'll watch developments from here, and send you word when to start them. Be ready in five minutes.'

The officer saluted, and as he wheeled his horse and galloped away, the general called after him: 'I don't think many of your mule drivers will get back.'

Henry and Wilson hurried back to the line, their faces showing how scared they were. As they came near, the lieutenant saw them, and shouted angrily: 'Fleming—Wilson—how long does it take you to get water. Where have you been?'

But he stopped when he saw the alarm in their eyes.

'We're going to charge. We're going to charge!' cried Wilson.

'Charge?' said the lieutenant. 'Charge? Well, by Gawd! Now, this is going to be real fighting. Charge? well, by Gawd!'

A small group of soldiers surrounded Henry and Wilson. 'Are we, really? Well, I'll be darned. Charge? What for? What at? Wilson, you're lying!'

'It's true,' Wilson replied angrily. 'Sure as hell, I tell you.' And Henry spoke up in support of him. 'Not on your life, he ain't lying. We heard 'em talking.'

Two mounted figures could be seen a short distance away. One was the colonel of the regiment, and the other was the officer who had received the orders from the general. Pointing at them, Wilson explained what he had heard.

One man had a final objection. 'How could you have heard 'em talking?' But most of the men believed it. They settled back into attitudes of waiting. Many tightened their belts and hitched up their trousers.

A moment later, the officers began to bustle about among the men, and to group them into a tighter formation. They chased any stragglers, like shepherds rounding up sheep.

Presently the regiment was ready, the soldiers bending forward like sprinters waiting the starting gun. And all around, the noise of the guns told of the wider struggle between the two armies, while the regiment concentrated on its own immediate, but smaller affair.

Henry shot a quick enquiring glance at his friend, and Wilson returned his look. They were the two who had secret knowledge: 'Mule drivers—hell to pay—don't believe many will get back.' But they saw no hesitation in each other's faces, and they nodded agreement when a man near them said, 'We'll get slaughtered.'

Chapter 19

Henry stared at the woods in front of him. The trees seemed to be hiding horrors and dangers. He knew that the orders had been given to start the charge, and he saw an officer—a mere boy on horseback—gallop up to the line and wave his hat.

The line seemed to fall forward with a gasp that was meant for a cheer. The regiment began its journey forward.

Henry was pushed for a moment; then he obeyed the general movement and began to run forward. He ran desperately, as if pursued. His eyes were fixed on a distant clump of trees and his face was hard and tight with his great effort. With his soiled uniform, his bandage, his wildly swinging rifle, and bumping kit at his waist, he looked a wild soldier indeed.

The line of men went straight at first, then its right wing lurched forward, to be in turn passed by the left, then the centre went to the front, until the regiment was a wedge-shaped mass of men.

Shells and bullets were all around. One man fell with his hands shielding his eyes. Other men fell in agonies, until there was a trail of bodies on the ground as the line ran forward.

It seemed to Henry that he saw everything bold and clear. His mind noted everything except what he himself was doing there.

Then the leaders slackened their speed; the regiment temporarily ceased to advance. The men saw some of their comrades dropping with moans and shrieks; some lay underfoot, still or wailing in distress. Many men stood with their rifles slack in their hands, watching the regiment dwindle. The sight seemed to overcome them with a paralysed sort of fascination.

There was a strange pause and a strange silence.

Then the lieutenant strode forth, his face black with rage: 'Come on, you fools!' he bellowed. 'Come on! You can't stay here. You must press on!' He said more, but it was not understood.

The men started firing again and moved uncertainly forward. Here, crouching behind trees, they looked over an open space that was exposed to enemy fire. As they halted, the lieutenant shouted at them again, swearing and coaxing.

He grabbed Henry's arm. 'Come on, block-head. We'll all get killed if we stay here. We've only got to get across there and—oh, come on!'

Henry looked at the officer in doubt. 'Cross *there*?' he said.

'We can't stay here,' screamed the lieutenant. 'Come on! We must get across!'

He took hold of Henry as if he would drag him forward. But the youth shook him off. 'Come on yourself, then!' he yelled.

They ran together down a slope. Wilson and several other men began to follow and yell, 'Come on—come on!'

The flag wavered for a moment and then was swept onward. Over the field went the handful of men into the face of the enemy. Henry ran like a madman, hoping to reach the woods before a bullet could find him. He ducked his head like a footballer and ran desperately on.

As he ran forward, a desperate love of the flag was all he thought of. It was a goddess—red and white—a woman that called to him with a voice of inspiration. He kept near the flag, as if it would be the saver of all their lives.

In the mad scramble he suddenly saw the **colour sergeant** flinch as if struck, and the man began to fall forward.

Henry sprang towards the flag and grabbed the pole. His friend saw this and immediately clutched at it from the other side. The colour sergeant, dying as he fell, was holding grimly on. In an instant of time, Henry and Wilson held the flag safely aloft as the dead man's hands fell away.

Chapter 20

The two youths, both holding the flag, now saw that many of the regiment lay dead, and that the rest were falling back. After their brave charge the men's strength was exhausted, and they were withdrawing to the shelter of the woods. The lieutenant tried vainly to rally them. 'Where in hell are you going?' he howled. Another officer shouted, 'Keep on shooting at 'em! Damn it!' There was much confusion as the men were given conflicting orders.

Henry and Wilson had a short tussle over the flag. 'Give it to me!' 'No, let me 'ave it!' Each wanted to show his willingness to take the risk of carrying the flag. But Henry, by pushing his friend aside, secured it for himself.

When the men reached the wood, they halted for some time, to fire at some enemy soldiers who were trailing them. Presently, they resumed their march under cover of the trees and bushes. By the time they reached an open space on the other side, they again came under heavy fire. There seemed to be enemy all around them.

Many of the men, their spirits faint after so much effort, began to feel they could carry on no longer. At the same time they had a suspicion that they had been betrayed, and they glared angrily at their officers.

However, there was a small body of men at the rear of the regiment, who were still determined to stand their ground. In command of them was the lieutenant. He had been shot in the arm, but this did not prevent him from shouting encouragement to his men, in spite of the awful pain of his wound.

Henry's dream of victory had vanished. Now the retreat had become for him a march of shame. He glared fiercely towards the enemy, but his hatred was concentrated on that officer, who, without knowing him, had called him a mule driver. He had even thought of writing an angry letter to him, saying 'So we are mule drivers, are we?' But as a result of the failure of the charge, he would look a fool if he did so. All he could do now, was to continue to appeal to his comrades not to lose heart. And in this he found support in the lieutenant, with whom he felt a sudden sense of fellowship and common purpose.

But the appeals of Henry and the lieutenant fell on deaf ears. Some of the men were slipping away, back to the lines. This began to weaken the resolve of the others; and all the time they were being fired at by the enemy, who now seemed to be surrounding them.

Henry boldly strode into the midst of the remaining men, and holding his flag aloft, took a defiant stand. Wilson came up to him and said, 'Well Henry, I guess this is good-bye!'

'Oh, shut up, you damn fool,' replied Henry, and would not even look at his friend.

The officers set about forming the men into a circle, to face the fire from whatever direction it might come. The ground was uneven, so that they were able to find a certain amount of cover. Low-lying mist and smoke prevented a clear view of their surroundings, and the men waited anxiously for it to lift.

Henry could see that the lieutenant was standing, sword in hand, keeping a very close watch. The smoky haze began slowly to drift, when the lieutenant suddenly yelled out: 'Here they come! Right on us, by Gawd!' Immediately the men responded with a savage burst of rifle fire.

As the mist cleared, a small body of enemy soldiers was revealed. They had been moving carefully forward, their rifles held in readiness, when the lieutenant spotted them. They were instantly recognised as enemy by the bright red facings on their light grey uniforms. The volley of fire from the men in blue stopped them in their tracks. It seemed that they must have been unaware how close they were to the lieutenant and his troop, or had missed their way. There was a rapid exchange of fire.

To Henry, seated on the ground with his flag firmly planted between his knees. the enemy seemed to be gaining ground. But he was sure that if they tried to capture his flag, they would have to pay dearly for it.

At last the enemy's fire grew slacker, and finally ceased altogether. As a breeze sprang up and blew away the mist and smoke, the men gazed upon the open space before them. No enemy could now be seen, except for a few bodies that lay twisted into unnatural shapes upon the ground.

The men sprang up from their cover, cheering them and dancing for joy. Not long before, they had seemed helpless and defeated. Now they had shown how well they could fight. They had revenged themselves upon their foes. They had regained their pride, and were filled with new enthusiasm. They were fighters. They were men!

Chapter 21

Suddenly they realised they were no longer threatened, and all ways open to them once more. The blue lines of their friends were near, and although there were loud noises in the distance, there was sudden stillness in this part of the field. Despite their reduced numbers they drew a breath of relief and gathered themselves into a bunch, and went on.

In this last stretch of the journey, they began to show strange emotions. Some hurried along in nervous fear, some showed an anxiety to find some sort of safety at all costs. It would be too bad to get killed now, after all they had been through.

As they approached their own lines, there was some sarcasm shouted from another regiment that was resting under some trees:

'Where the hell have you been?'

'What ya comin' back for?'

'Why didn't you stay there, then?'

'Was it warm out there, sonny?'

'Goin' home now, boys?'

One shouted in baby language: 'Oh, mama, come quick and look at the sojers!'

There was no reply from the bruised and battered regiment, save from one man who waved his fists in the air.

Henry resented the mocking voices. He shot a glance full of hate in their direction, but trudged on. When they arrived at their old position, they turned to look at the ground over which they had charged.

Henry saw that the distance was nothing. The trees were much nearer than he had thought, and the time taken, too, was much shorter. The crowded events had taken place much more quickly than seemed possible now.

The men were lying about on the ground, red-eyed, choking with dust, gulping at what water they still had, rubbing their faces with coat sleeves and bunches of grass.

But Henry was secretly pleased with his own performance during the charge. He had done better than he had expected.

As the regiment lay panting from its exertions, the officer who had called them mule drivers came along the line on his horse. He had lost his cap, his hair was tossed in the wind, and he was in a temper. This showed in the way he managed his horse. He jerked at the bridle, drawing up with a sharp pull near the colonel of the regiment. His voice came clearly to the listening men: 'By thunder, MacChesnay, what a bull you made of it! What a mess! Good Lord, man, you stopped them a hundred feet short of where you should have been! It would have been a great success, but as it is—well, what a lot of mud diggers you've got, anyway!'

The men waited to see what their colonel would reply to this. He wore an injured air, and put out a hand in protest. 'Oh, well, general, you know, we went as far as we could,' he said.

'As far as you could! Did you, by Gawd. Well, that wasn't very far, was it?' the general snorted. 'You were intended to make a diversion for Whiterside. Well, you can hear now how well you succeeded!' He wheeled his horse and rode away.

In the woods to the left a renewed barrage of fire broke out.

The lieutenant, who had heard all the remarks, was furious. 'I don't care who a man is, a general or what, but if he says the boys didn't put up a good charge, he's a fool!'

The colonel **reproved** him for this. 'This is my own affair, lieutenant,' he said, severely. 'It is not for you to . . .'

'All right, colonel, all right.'

Some of this got passed down the line of men. 'By thunder!' some of them were heard to say, 'What does the general want, then? Did he think we went out there and played marbles? He didn't see nothing of how we did. He thinks we're just a lot of sheep. He doesn't know what it was like . . . '

'It's a pity old Henderson got killed yesterday,' said Henry. 'He'd have known we did our best and fought good. It's just our awful luck, that's all.'

'I should say so,' added Wilson. 'There's no fun in fighting for people who are never pleased. We did our best sure enough. Next time they want us to charge, I bet I stay behind and let them go to the devil with it.'

Henry calmed his friend. 'We both did our best anyway, John. I'd like to see the fool who'd say we didn't.' Wilson went on: 'I heard one feller say we two did about the best of any of the regiment. Well, we did fight like thunder; I don't care who hears me say it. But those old soldiers—tittering and laughing—I can't stand them, and that old general—well, he's just crazy.'

Henry shouted, 'He makes me mad. He's a block-head! I wish he'd come along with us next time. We'd show 'im . . . '

Just then several men came hurrying up bringing news.

'Oh, Flem, you oughta heard,' cried one.

'Heard what?' said Henry.

'You just oughta heard!' was repeated, as a circle of men gathered round. 'Well, the colonel met your lieutenant right by us—it was the darndest thing I ever heard—"Oh," he says, "Mr Hasbrook, by the way, who was that lad what carried the flag?" he says, and the lieutenant, he speaks up right away, "That's Fleming, and he's a right jimhickey," he says. Those were his words—a right jimhickey—and the colonel says, "Huh, huh—he's a good man indeed,—huh, huh—he kept the flag way out in front, I saw him!" "You bet," says the lieutenant, "he and a fellow called Wilson were ahead of the charge, howling like Indians all the time, they were, ahead of the charge." And the colonel says, "What, those two babies?—well they deserve to be major-generals—sure—they deserve to be major-generals!" '

Henry and his friend said: 'Huh! You're lying. He never said that? Oh, what a lie!' But they were both flushed with pleasure in spite of the playful scorn of their fellows. They exchanged a secret glance of joy and pride. This made it all worth while.

They speedily forgot the many errors and disappointments of the past, and gave way to happy satisfaction. Their hearts were full of grateful affection for their colonel and the youthful lieutenant, and for what had been overheard.

Chapter 22

During the brief period of rest which now followed, Henry was able to watch the progress of the battle. Large numbers of the enemy were now pouring out of the woods, to the right and left of the line. From where Henry stood, he could watch the attack begin against a section of the blue line on the side of a nearby hill.

Not far away, in an open space, as if set apart from the rest, two regiments from each side were engaged in a **ding-dong** fight. These four regiments seemed to be staging a contest quite separate from the main struggle—rather as if they were taking part in a match for a **wager**.

In another direction a brigade in fine order could be seen advancing, evidently intending to drive the enemy from a wood. They passed in and out of Henry's view, and presently loud bursts of firing could be heard. But, apparently finding their task too difficult, the brigade soon came marching out again with its fine formation undisturbed.

On a slope to the left there was a long row of big guns firing their shells at the enemy, who were forming for another attack in the unending conflict. Amid the red flashes and the thick smoke from the guns, groups of toiling artillery men could be seen. Behind the guns, stood a house, calm and white amid the bursting shells sent over from the enemy guns. A row of horses, tied to a long railing, tugged frantically at their bridles.

Meanwhile, the separate battle between the four regiments lasted for some time, until the rebels faltered and drew back. The two dark blue regiments could be heard shouting in triumph, and Henry could see their two flags being waved in celebration of their victory.

Presently there was an **ominous** stillness. The blue lines shifted position and regrouped. They stared expectantly at the silent woods and fields before them.

On a hill opposite a desperate struggle was taking place. Two waves of infantry faced each other, swinging to and fro. Sometimes, one side seemed to claim victory by its yells and cheers, only to be answered by yells and cheers from the other. As the battle flags were continually being carried this way and that, Henry could not tell which side was winning.

Soon the time came for his regiment, reduced in strength though it was, to be sent again into action. The men re-entered the fight fiercely and with determination. Their rifles flashed yellow and red through the smoke wall their firing created. With their faces black with smoke, their eyes glowing and their bodies swaying, they looked like strange and ugly devils, clumsily dancing in the smoke.

Henry, still the bearer of the colours, was a fascinated spectator. He leaned forward, talking to himself, uttering words of encouragement. The lieutenant, too, urged the men on with his usual store of oaths.

But a formidable line of the enemy had come dangerously close. They quickly gained the protection of a fence, and sliding down behind it began to pour forth a murderous fire at the blue line.

The men of the 304th regiment now braced themselves for a great struggle. Henry resolved not to **budge**, whatever happened. He could not forget the officer who had called them 'mule drivers' and later on, 'mud diggers'. He would die at his post, and the sight of his dead body on the field would be, to that officer, a lasting reproach.

There were heavy casualties. Many were shot dead, and fell at the feet of their comrades. Some of the wounded managed to crawl away, but others lay where they were shot, vainly struggling to get up. The orderly sergeant was shot in the face. Henry saw him struggle to the rear, his jaw hanging down, his mouth a mass of blood.

Henry looked around for Wilson. He saw a young man, smeared with gun-powder, whom he knew at once to be his friend. The lieutenant, also, was unharmed, still continuing to curse and swear. But it was now with the air of a man who had exhausted both his strength and his vocabulary.

The fire of the regiment was beginning to slacken, and their will to resist was rapidly failing.

Chapter 23

The colonel came running along at the back of the line. Other officers followed him. 'We must charge 'em!' they shouted. 'We must charge 'em!' they repeated, as if they half expected the men would refuse to obey such an order.

When Henry heard this, he began to judge the distance between him and the enemy. He saw that they must go forward again. Their only hope was to **dislodge** the enemy from their position behind the fence.

He expected that his companions, weary and stiff after the recent fight, would have to be driven hard to attack again. But he was surprised to find that they were just as keen as he was. As the order to charge was given, the soldiers sprang eagerly forward towards the fence.

Henry kept the bright colours of the flag well to the front. He waved his free arm furiously, all the time uttering wild calls and appeals, but those who followed him needed no encouragement. They, too, were wild with enthusiasm, and seemed to have no fear.

As they came near the fence, it seemed certain that many must die on the field before they reached their goal. Henry felt like a wild savage in a religous frenzy. He strained all his strength. He could feel the onward surge of the regiment about him, and pictured the thunderous blow that would crush the enemy. This vision made him run faster than his comrades, who were all the time shouting and cheering behind him.

Presently, Henry saw that many of the rebels did not intend to wait for the attack. He could see a number of them turn and run. But at one part of their line there was a small group standing firm. They were settled behind the posts and rails of the fence. Over them their flag waved defiantly, and their rifles spat fire.

The men in blue were now very close to their foes. Insults and angry shouts were exchanged, as the distance between the two sides was reduced to only a few paces.

Henry had fixed his gaze on the enemy's flag. Possession of it would be his proudest moment. He plunged madly towards it, his own flag waving above him.

The charging body of blue men suddenly halted at close range, and fired a swift volley. The group in grey was split and broken by this fire, and the men in blue yelled and rushed in upon them.

Henry saw four or five of the enemy stretched upon the ground, as if they had been struck by a bolt from the sky. **Tottering** among them was the rival colour bearer, who had been **mortally** wounded by the last deadly volley. His face was ghastly pale, but on it was a look of desperate purpose. With terrible resolution he hugged his precious flag to his chest, and was trying to stagger away to safety. But his wounds were too severe, and when the blue men leaped over the fence there was despair in his eyes, as he glanced back at them.

Wilson cleared the fence with a great leap, and springing at the flag, wrenched it free from the dying man's grasp. The colour bearer fell to the ground, and with a final cry, turned his dead face to the ground. There was much blood upon the grass.

At one part of the line four men had been taken prisoner. Some blue men surrounded them, and were examining them as if they were caged animals.

One of the prisoners had a slight wound in his foot, which he was examining. He looked up to curse his captors, as if they were clumsy intruders who had trodden on his toe. Another was a mere boy, who suffered his capture with great calmness and good nature. A third sat with a defiant expression on his face. If anything was said to him, he would only reply, 'Ah, go to hell!' The last of the four prisoners never spoke. He thought only of the shame of being captured, regretting that he had lost the right to resist.

After a celebration of their success, the men of the 304th settled down behind the fence. There was some long grass in which Henry rested, supporting the flag against a railing. Wilson, overjoyed and holding his treasure, came to join his friend. They sat side by side, and congratulated each other.

Chapter 24

The roarings in the forest began to grow weaker. Artillery could still be heard in the distance, but rifle fire had almost ceased.

Henry and Wilson looked up suddenly, almost missing the sound of those noises that had become a part of their life. There were changes going on among the troops—marching this way and that way.

Henry got up. 'Well, what now, I wonder?' He shaded his eyes and gazed into the distance.

John Wilson also got up. 'I bet we're going to get out of this place, and back over the river,' he said.

'Well, I don't know,' Henry said. They waited, watching.

Soon, orders came that the regiment was to return to its former position. The men got up, grunting and grumbling at having to leave their rest. Their legs were stiff, and they stretched their arms over their heads. One man swore as he rubbed his eyes. They all groaned, 'Oh, Lord!'

They tramped slowly back over the field across which they had run so fast not long before. The fence was deserted now. Beyond it lay a few dead soldiers. Among them was clearly seen the colour-bearer in grey, whose flag Wilson was now carrying.

The regiment soon rejoined the brigade in column, and they became a mass of dust-covered troops, marching parallel to the enemy's lines they had seen in the previous action.

They passed near a white house, and saw in front of it groups of their comrades lying in wait behind an earthwork. A row of guns was booming away at a distant enemy. Shells were falling in reply, raising dust and splinters. Horsemen dashed along the line.

The division began to curve away from the field, and went off in the direction of the river. When Henry noticed this he breathed a sigh of satisfaction. 'Well, it's all over,' he said to Wilson.

His friend gazed behind them. 'By Gawd, it is,' he agreed.

Henry reflected about events on the battlefield. He had been in a world of shot and shell fire, and at last he had come out of it. He had seen blood and passion, and he had escaped death. As he thought of his deeds, failures and achievements, he decided that he had not done badly on the whole.

Wilson, too, seemed to be thinking back over the battle, and then he suddenly cried, 'Good Lord!'

'What?' asked Henry.

'Good Lord!' repeated Wilson. 'You know Jimmy Rogers—well—he was hurt and—gosh, I started to get some water for him, and—by thunder—I've not seen him from that day to this! I clean forgot—say—has anybody seen Jimmy Rogers?'

'Seen 'im? No, he's dead,' they told him.

Wilson swore.

Henry was remembering some of his deeds in action with a certain amount of pleasure and pride. He remembered some of the praise he'd had. He reminded himself of the lieutenant's words that gave him such a thrill. 'If I'd had ten thousand wild cats like you, I could finish off this war in less than a week!' Henry would never forget that.

Nevertheless, there was the fact of his running away from that first battle. That still made him feel a sense of shame. Many of his fellows had run too—that was natural—but that was no excuse.

But yet at the back of his mind, the knowledge that he had deserted the tattered soldier remained. To leave a man, who had been so anxious about Henry's 'hurt'— who had needed his help, only to be deserted at last, while Henry went off on his own! He had been wrong. It was an error that would remain with him all his life. It was a mistake he could not forgive in himself. It was not redeemed, even by his other deeds of courage and success.

He wondered if his companions guessed that he had this weight on his mind, but they were all plodding along discussing events in the recent battle.

'Oh, if you ask me, I'd say we got a damn good licking!'

'Licking! No, we ain't licked, sonny. We're going down here, swinging around, and we'll come in behind 'em.'

'Oh, I've seen all I want to see. Don't tell me about comin' in behind . . . '

'Bill Smithers, he ses he's rather be in a hundred battles than in that helluva hospital. He ses there was shooting all the night-time, and shells dropped even on the hospital. He ses he never did hear such hollering.'

'Hasbrook? He's the best officer we've got. He's a whale!' 'Didn't I tell you we'd come in behind 'em?'

Henry took no part in this chatter. He was still thinking about the tattered soldier and his desertion of him, besides his own weakness in giving way to panic in the first battle. But even to himself he still did not fully admit his worst sin—which was to lie about his wound, and how it happened. It took a good deal of courage to realise the failures and disappointments of warfare, and his own behaviour in the past few days most of all.

But gradually Henry was able to set his sins at a distance and look ahead. He saw the world with new eyes, and he began to realise that there are blessings to be had in new strength, a new determination to be a man.

So it came to pass that as he trudged from the battlefield he could feel a sense of peace. He had rid himself of the red sickness of battle. Ahead of him were peaceful skies, fresh meadows and cool brooks.

Over the river a golden ray of sunshine came through the grey of the rain-clouds.

. . . .

Glossary

1   *reluctantly*: not eagerly

    orderlies: soldiers who attend an officer

    herald of signal importance: messenger of noteworthy news

    mournfully: sadly

2   *ain't*:   is not, isn't (used by the uneducated in conversation)

    bustled about: behaved importantly

    care a hang: not care at all

3   *patriotism*:   love of country

    checking of his ambitions: halting the achievement of plans

4   *brindle*:   brownish with streaks of other colour

    lick: (slang) defeat

5   *likker*:   (slang) liquor, that is, alcohol

    thronged: crowd round

    martial: warlike

6   *basked*:   enjoy or revel in light or warmth

    monotony: boredom

    Yank: Yankee, or someone from northern USA

    haversack: stout bag carried on the back or over the shoulders by soldiers

7   *unknown quantity*:   untested

8   *exasperated*:   very irritated

    Richmond: a city in Virginia about 160 kms SSW of Washington, D.C., and first capital of the Confederacy

Johnies: a nickname for the Confederate soldiers

Chapter 2
10   *sound out*:   find out (from 'sounding' water to find its depth)

sharing his confidence: telling a private matter with trust

instinctively: naturally, without thought

11   *drew rein*:   the stopping of a horse by pulling on the reins

14   *thunderin' peeked*:   (slang) very tired

short rations: too little food

15   *thump*:   (slang) hit

skedaddled: (slang) ran away

Chapter 3
17   *pontoon bridge*:   a temporary bridge made by putting planks or boards across a row of floating small boats

18   *standard-bearer*:   flag carrier

croon: sing softly

19   *skirmishers*:   men in small parties who engage in a piece of irregular or unplanned fighting

21   *skulking*:   moving in a sneaky fashion, often to avoid danger

rampart: wall made of earth as a defence

Chapter 4
25   *on picket*:   on sentry duty

26   *creek*:   a stream or break in the sea-coast

27   *stampede*:   sudden fright and scattering of horses, cattle or people

chaos: confusion

Chapter 5

29   *fraternity*:   brotherhood; a group of men sharing common goals and ideals

31   *reproach*:   blame

    stoker in a foundry: a workman who puts fuel, usually coal, into a furnace

    squat: here, to crouch down low, the feet flat on the ground

Chapter 6

34   *endurance*:   ability to bear pain or suffering with self-control or courage

    perseverance: ability to carry on despite difficulties

35   *irresistible*:   too tempting or strong not to give way to

38   *chestnut*:   reddish-brown; from the colour of the nut of the chestnut tree

    wallop: defeat

    spurred: urge (a horse) forward by pressing a spur on a boot into the animal's flank

Chapter 7

41   *heeding*:   paying attention to (a warning, advice, etc)

    sanctuary: holy or sacred place, usually in a church, from which you could not be taken or arrested

Chapter 8

42   *awestruck*:   suddenly filled with awe, wonder, surprise

    medley: a mixture of different things

44   *sulkily*:   with silent bad temper

45   *tattered*:   ragged

Chapter 22

92   *ding-dong*:   (slang) slam-bang; something vigorous

      wager: bet

      ominous: frightening

93   *budge*:   move

Chapter 23

94   *dislodge*:   move someone or something from a particular or fixed place

95   *tottering*:   staggering

      mortally: fatally